KT-547-997

MONTANA

Welcome to Montana—a place of passion and adventure, where there is a charming little town with some big secrets…

Josh Anderson: This sexy contractor found himself flat on his back with Lori Hanson's grip on his throat. What a way to fall...in love. And nothing would stop him from finding out her secrets—or winning her heart!

Lori Hanson: This reclusive beauty has hands that should be registered as lethal weapons. Though on the run from danger, she can't hide her growing attraction to her boss, Josh Anderson...or the fact that she's having trouble concentrating on her work.

Melissa North: Why do strange things keep happening to her? And why does newcomer Lori Hanson seem so familiar to her?

Homer Gilmore: The man wanders around town lost in his own world, but carrying a burden that no one can see. Does he know the person who's been causing trouble around Whitehorn?

Dear Reader,

Welcome in the New Year with six wonderful, warm, emotional stories from Special Edition.

The second story in our latest MONTANA series pops up this month with *In Love With Her Boss* by Christie Ridgway. Look out for the next instalment from Jackie Merritt in February.

Popular author Joan Elliott Pickart shows us how great it is to have kids in *Single with Twins*, while Gina Wilkins says that sometimes it's the best man, *not* the groom, who gets the girl in *The Groom's Stand-In*.

Meanwhile, Jennifer Mikels gives her heroine *The Child She Always Wanted* as part of her FAMILY REVELATIONS series—look out for her next story in March. Victoria Pade gives us a story with a twist with *On Pins and Needles* as her A RANCHING FAMILY series continues; and Christine Flynn shows how a man and a woman can work together even when they take on the task of looking after *Another Man's Children*.

We hope you enjoy them all.

Happy New Year!

The Editors

In Love With
Her Boss

CHRISTIE RIDGWAY

SILHOUETTE®
SPECIAL EDITION™

For Barbara Freethy, a great listener. Thanks.

DID YOU PURCHASE THIS BOOK WITHOUT A COVER?

If you did, you should be aware it is **stolen property** as it was reported *unsold and destroyed* by a retailer. Neither the author nor the publisher has received any payment for this book.

All the characters in this book have no existence outside the imagination of the author, and have no relation whatsoever to anyone bearing the same name or names. They are not even distantly inspired by any individual known or unknown to the author, and all the incidents are pure invention.

All Rights Reserved including the right of reproduction in whole or in part in any form. This edition is published by arrangement with Harlequin Enterprises II B.V. The text of this publication or any part thereof may not be reproduced or transmitted in any form or by any means, electronic or mechanical, including photocopying, recording, storage in an information retrieval system, or otherwise, without the written permission of the publisher.

This book is sold subject to the condition that it shall not, by way of trade or otherwise, be lent, resold, hired out or otherwise circulated without the prior consent of the publisher in any form of binding or cover other than that in which it is published and without a similar condition including this condition being imposed on the subsequent purchaser.

Silhouette, Silhouette Special Edition and Colophon are registered trademarks of Harlequin Books S.A., used under licence.

*First published in Great Britain 2003
Silhouette Books, Eton House, 18-24 Paradise Road,
Richmond, Surrey TW9 1SR*

© Harlequin Books S.A. 2002

Special thanks and acknowledgement are given to Christie Ridgway for her contribution to the Montana series.

ISBN 0 373 24441 X

23-0103

*Printed and bound in Spain
by Litografia Rosés S.A., Barcelona*

CHRISTIE RIDGWAY

thinks she has the greatest job in the world. She loves writing stories, and the only thing she loves more is her family: a supportive husband and two sons who often are forced to remind her that kids are entitled to three meals a day!

A native of California, she now lives in the southern part of the state. A typical writing day can include rescuing the turtle from the pool and finding frogs in the shower. Although she once told the men she loves they could not keep pets that require live food, each week her husband comes home with a plastic bag of pet food that looks suspiciously like crickets (sounds like them, too!) for the reptiles and amphibians that now call her home theirs.

When not writing or chasing down errant pets, she volunteers at her sons' school. Finally, because there's really nothing better, Christie always finds time to curl up with a good book.

You may contact her at PO Box 3803, La Mesa, CA 91944, USA. Send an SAE with return postage for a reply, or e-mail her at christie@christieridgway.com

SILHOUETTE®
SPECIAL EDITION™

*presents six more passionate and
adventurous stories from*

MONTANA

*Welcome to Montana—a place of passion
and adventure, where there is a charming
little town with some big secrets...*

Chapter One

The calendar read December twenty-fourth, but Lori Hanson wanted to forget all about Christmas. She wanted to forget a lot of things, truth to tell, which was why she was impatient to begin her workout at the state-of-the-art facility located at Whitehorn High School in Whitehorn, Montana. Standing in the small entry area, she clutched her gym bag in one hand and used the other to dig in her coat pocket for her membership card.

Card located, she stepped up to the desk, ignoring the Christmas carols piping cheerfully through the speakers, the red-and-green tinsel draped along the counter, the fuzzy Santa hat perched on the head of the high-school boy who was there to check her in. His winning smile was impossible to avoid, though. "Merry Christmas," he said.

"You, too," Lori murmured, hoping her Scrooge mood didn't show. But Christmas was for families, something she didn't have in Whitehorn...not yet.

The boy took her card and wrote her name down in a ledger book. "New member?" he asked.

"Yes, I sure am." She'd only been in Whitehorn a week, but she'd joined the gym the day after finding her small apartment and hours after she'd gone shopping for a winter-in-Montana wardrobe and groceries. To Lori, working out had become a necessity on a par with shelter, clothing and food.

"Texas?" the high-schooler asked as he handed back her card.

Lori frowned. "Texas?"

"Your accent." The boy grinned. "My mom loves to watch those *Dallas* reruns."

"Oh. No. I'm from South Carolina." But she was never going back there. She couldn't.

"South Carolina." His forehead scrunched in thought, he leaned back in his chair. "Capital city, Columbia, population approximately 4 million, major economic features are textile manufacturing, tourism and agriculture."

At Lori's clear surprise, he grinned again. "County geography champ last year."

This time Lori had to grin back, because his big, open smile was that cute. When she was in high school she would certainly have fallen in love with a boy like this one. Then her smile faded. Those years were long gone, though, and when she *had* fallen in love it was with a man who had kept his true nature hidden. She shoved her card back in her pocket and turned toward the women's locker room.

The boy wasn't through with her, though. "Winter in Montana's going to be a shock," he advised.

She sent him a half-smile over her shoulder, but kept on walking. She'd been shocked before. She had come to Montana in winter to get away from all that. To make a new start.

The locker room was deserted. Probably most women were completing their last-minute Christmas shopping or putting the finishing touches on a big family meal. Lori stifled a sharp pang of loneliness and focused instead on shedding her heavy outer clothing and exchanging her winter boots for her running shoes. The sooner she started running, the sooner she could forget her troubles.

The weight room was nearly empty too, but on its other side there was a basketball game in progress on one of the courts surrounding the indoor running track. She paused, out of long habit cautiously surveying the men at play.

Though they were the right age, somewhere in their thirties, none of them had the lean, almost slight build of the man she was constantly on watch for. Thank God.

Relaxing, she continued watching for a minute. Goodness, the males grew big in Montana. The players on the court were all over six feet tall—one of them probably six and a half feet!—with heavy shoulders and broad chests to match.

In various examples of ragged workout wear, they

sweated and grunted and thundered up and down the court, trading good-natured insults. Lori finally moved her gaze from them and walked onto the gray-surfaced track. Eager to begin, she had to force herself to stretch before running. Shoulders, hamstrings, calves: she methodically warmed them up.

A harsh shout from the basketball court caused her to flinch—raised voices still did that to her—but she made herself complete her final stretches. Then, only then, did she allow herself to start running.

Aaaah. It was almost a physical sigh that rippled through her mind as she began. A year ago, when she'd taken up running, it had merely been a part of an overall conditioning routine that she'd used to get control over her life. Self-defense classes, some weight training, the running, they were ways to gain confidence.

But the running had gained her something else, too. A runner's high. The zone, as she described it to herself. It was a place where the past couldn't find her and where she could calmly escape her present worries as well.

Even now, the murals painted on the walls of the gym began to blur. They were beautiful scenes of Montana, wildflowers, snow on the Crazy Mountains, elk on rugged plains, but as her pace increased their colors blurred. The mingled sounds of "Jingle Bells" and the thud of the basketball against wood receded too, and Lori's mood lifted.

She was safe here. Safe in the zone. Safe in Montana. It was right to come back to her mother's hometown. The day after Christmas she'd start her temporary job. And some days after that, she'd begin on the real task that had brought her here to Whitehorn.

Her speed picked up another notch, and she felt her long hair fluttering against the back of her neck. In South Carolina, she'd run outdoors, and even in the zone she'd run with one eye looking over her shoulder at all times. In Montana it was going to be different.

The hair at her temples dampened, though the breeze her own movement created dried the sweat on her face. She reveled in the pumping motion of her arms and legs, in her escalating mood, in—

A body bumped into Lori from behind. Impressions flashed through her mind.

Huge. Heavy breath. Grasping hands.

Panic speared her. Her feet skittered forward. Strong fingers bit into her arms. She was jerked upright, back.

Then survival instincts woke. A burst of adrenaline surged through her muscles. With desperate strength, she tried pulling free of her assailant. Both off-balance, their feet tangled. They pitched forward. Lori landed belly-down on the running surface, the man half on top of her.

Even with the breath knocked out of her, two years of self-defense classes exploded into action. *No! Not this time!* Lori's mind screamed.

With a frantic twist, she heaved off his weight. Leverage on her side now, she threw herself over him, her forearm across his throat. Gulping one desperate breath, she tossed her hair out of her face and looked down into his eyes. Into the eyes of…

A stranger. A dark-eyed, dark-haired stranger.

Aghast, yet still half-afraid, Lori jumped up, then backed away from the massive form lying on the ground like a felled tree. Male laughter rang out, and she glanced around, bewildered. The basketball game had halted and the players were looking at her.

No, at him.

He was looking at her.

His face, all angles made up of strong cheekbones and a chiseled jaw, appeared rough-hewn, handsome, even when slightly dazed. His eyes were bittersweet-chocolate brown with long black lashes she'd have had to use two coats of mascara to achieve. He blinked, as if trying to clear his head.

Lori swallowed, a new kind of alarm zinging through her. "I'm so sorry. Are you…are you all right?"

He didn't move. "Depends on if you're asking me or my ego."

She swallowed again. "What?"

He seemed to consider a moment. "Okay. The answer is, I'm fine, but the ego might need a good soak in the whirlpool." His mouth lifted in the slowest, sweetest smile Lori had ever seen in her life. "Join me?" he asked.

She took a giant step back. "No."

"But it's Christmas." His crestfallen expression made her feel as if she'd stolen the ribbon from around a teddy bear's neck.

Then he rose to his feet, and she just felt afraid. The basketball player she'd attacked was the huge one she'd noticed earlier. He towered over her five feet eight inches and, as he came toward her, Lori found herself retreating farther.

Her heart slammed against her chest as he just kept coming. She scuttled back some more.

"Watch—" he started, reaching out.

Too late. Her feet tripped over a basketball. With resigned dismay, she realized she was falling again. His huge hand came nearer, as if to catch her, and by some miracle—fear over physics—she managed to regain her balance before he could touch her. She felt her face flush.

"Are you all right?" he asked.

Lori couldn't remember the last time she'd been so clumsy. "It depends on if you're asking me or my ego."

At her little joke, he smiled again, slow and big. "I'm Josh," he said, bending to retrieve the ball.

"Lori," she answered, moving back another step.

Catcalls from the court had him glancing over her head and he tossed the basketball toward his teammates. "I'm sorry, Lori. The first apology should have been mine. I was chasing after the ball and didn't look where I was going."

Her breathing could finally settle down, but, funny, it didn't. "I'm sorry too. I…overreacted."

He shrugged, his massive shoulders moving up and down. "Can't believe a little thing like you could overturn me like that."

She half smiled. "I'm stronger than I look." That was her hope, anyway.

The other men were shouting at him from the court. Lori glanced over her shoulder. "I think they want you to rejoin the game. You're sure you're not hurt?" Her face heated again as their tangle replayed in her mind. The man probably thought she was certifiable for going into maul-the-mugger-mode at the slightest contact.

He shook his head. "I'm fine. You might considering registering with the sheriff as a lethal weapon, though."

Her eyebrows rose. "My hands, you mean?"

His eyebrows lifted, too. "The whole package, sweetheart." With another of those slow smiles warming his rugged face, he touched two fingers to his forehead in a casual salute and then jogged back to his game.

Struck dumb by his good looks and almost offhand charm, Lori found herself staring after him. She was still standing there three baskets later, when despite his large size, he made a graceful, clean *swish* of two points and glanced over at her, grinning in triumph.

With a jerk, Lori got herself moving again, even as yet another blush crawled up her neck to her cheeks. Steering way clear of the game, she headed for the locker room.

There were some things it wasn't smart to forget, not even for a moment. South Carolina hadn't been safe because of a man. She wasn't going to let the same thing happen to her here in Montana.

By the time she was back in her outerwear, she was feeling a lot less flustered. She hadn't seen Josh at the gym before today, and she probably never would see him again. If she did, she'd ignore him. That would be simple enough.

The day after Christmas, Lori braked her car in front of a small building and opened her notebook to recheck the address she was seeking. Though a small sign declared the place was indeed Anderson, Inc., the site of her temporary job, the dark-red, wood-sided building looked more like an old schoolhouse than the office of a construction company.

But the address was the correct one, so she parked her car in the small attached lot beside a behemoth four-wheel-drive SUV, then headed for the front door. Her black boots made quiet *clacks* against the brick pathway. She'd teamed the boots with a long black wool skirt and a chunky black sweater. An austere look, maybe, but warm. Her roots might be in Montana, but her leaves were definitely more accustomed to the milder Southern winters.

Despite her woolen clothing, a small shiver rolled down her spine. But it was normal apprehension, not a quaking, stomach-knotting fear, thank God. She was starting the first job of her new life today, and she desperately wanted it to go smoothly.

Through the plate-glass front door, Lori spied the orangey curls of Lucy Meyer. The fortyish woman was a new mom and Lori had been hired to replace her as the receptionist while Lucy took maternity leave. They'd met once—in Lucy's home. Her baby had just arrived—a month early—and Lucy was anxious to get someone to help "the boss" as she referred to the head of the company, Mr. Anderson, as soon as possible.

When Lori opened the door, Lucy turned toward her with a smile. "Come in, come in," the other woman said, bustling forward with characteristic energy.

Lori walked into an expansive reception area. Centered on the wall to her right sat a woodburning stove that was pumping out pleasant heat. A large oval rag rug, in shades of red and cream, covered a honey-toned wooden floor. Several comfortable-looking chairs and a selection of magazines made the room appear even more homey.

Lucy took Lori's coat and hung it on one of the brass hooks attached to the wall by the door. "I want to get you as familiar with things as I can before the squeaker gets hungry," she said.

Lori smiled, her nervousness allayed by the unexpected pleasantness of the office. "Where is Baby Walt?"

Lucy jerked her head in the direction of a doorway off the waiting area. "With the boss. I'll introduce you to him in a minute."

Lori had only a second to peer through the indicated door, and only another to absorb a glimpse of a massive desk with a pair of giant-sized, booted feet propped atop it. Then Lucy drew her away.

"This is where you sit," she said. Centered a few

feet from the front door was an old wooden desk that looked as if it had once belonged to a schoolmistress. A computer and state-of-the-art phone system on its top appeared efficient, though anachronistic.

Lori took notes as Lucy explained the workings of the phone and the small amount of computer work the receptionist's job entailed. Then she followed the other woman down a short hall that led to a bathroom, a large conference area and an almost-closet that held a refrigerator and coffeemaker.

They were standing in the filing-cum-supply room when Lucy suddenly stilled. ''Uh-oh,'' she said. ''The squeaker. I'd better go rescue the boss.''

As they exited the room, Lori could hear the baby fussing herself, and a man's deep voice trying to soothe him. Then the baby and man noises sounded louder, as if both were coming toward Lori and Lucy. Lori straightened her shoulders and smoothed her skirt, hoping she was going to like Mr. Anderson as much as she liked his office space.

Lori and Lucy turned the corner into the reception area, coming face-to-face with Baby Walt and Mr. Anderson. Lori stiffened.

Apparently Mr. Anderson was Mr. *Josh* Anderson. Lori's Josh.

Not *her* Josh, she amended hastily, but that mammoth Josh she'd hoped never to see again. Just that morning, she'd been relieved not to run in to him— figuratively or literally—when she'd worked out at the gym right after dawn.

His eyebrows rose in mild surprise as he transferred

the baby to his mother's arms. "Who's your new friend?" he asked Lucy over the child's fussing.

Lucy had eyes only for the baby. "She's *your* new receptionist. I told you she was coming in today. Josh Anderson, this is Lori Hanson."

"We've met," he said.

That caught Lucy's attention. She looked up. "What?"

Lori tried to think what to do. Even with five feet separating them, Josh was so big. Too big. And her heart was pumping too hard. "I—"

She clamped her mouth shut on her immediate urge to say she couldn't take the position after all. The temporary agency she'd signed with wouldn't be exactly thrilled if she couldn't stay on the job for even an hour. "We met at the gym," she told Lucy.

The other woman's gaze sharpened. "Really? How—" The baby wailed louder, and Lucy broke off to change his position. Then she looked over at Josh, her expression rueful. "I'm taking Lori through the files, and the squeaker's noise is going to echo like crazy off the metal cabinets. I recommend you take an hour's coffee break—at least a block away."

Some of the tension left Lori's shoulders. With Josh out of the office, she could pump Lucy for information about him and then decide if she could really take on this assignment.

But Josh was shaking his head. "I'm expecting some plans to be dropped off."

Lori let out a slow breath. Okay, so he'd still be around. But in the privacy of the filing room, she knew that the talkative Lucy would be happy to give an honest assessment of her boss.

The baby wiggled and cried louder. Josh reached out his enormous hand and ran it over the back of the baby's fuzzy head. "Luce, why don't you take Walt home? I can show Lori what she needs to know."

"Oh, but—" Another infant wail interrupted Lucy's protest. "I think I will," she said, with a grateful smile. "If you don't mind, Lori?"

As if she could ask a new mother to put off taking her unhappy infant home. Smiling weakly, Lori shook her head. "I'll be fine with Mr. Anderson."

"Josh," he said. "Just Josh."

"I'll be fine," she echoed obediently, thinking of his big hand on the baby's tiny head. "With Josh." Wouldn't she?

In the few minutes it took for Lucy to gather her things, though, Lori's nervousness grew. When the front door shut behind the other woman, its thud was nothing compared to the loud, anxious thumping of her heart.

But she could do this, she thought, sitting down in the receptionist's chair and pulling her notebook and pencil front and center. It didn't matter that he was standing on the other side of her desk and that they were alone in the office. It didn't matter that he was big. That he was young and good-looking. He was just her boss.

Keep it impersonal, she told herself. They'd concentrate their attention on files, phone calls, blueprints. Business.

Her eyes focused in the vicinity of the second button of the denim workshirt he was wearing with a pair of clean but worn jeans, she made her voice brisk. "Where would you like to start?"

"I keep thinking I've seen you somewhere before."

Her gaze jumped to his. His dark eyebrows were drawn together over his dark brown eyes. His coffee-colored hair was slightly shaggy. Its ends brushed against his collar as he shook his head. "You're familiar."

Uneasiness drew like a cold finger down her spine. "The gym," she said, her mouth dry.

He shook his head again. "No. Somewhere else... someone else?"

She didn't want him pursuing that line of thought. "But I've never been to Montana before." Except for the first few weeks following her conception. "Have you ever been to South Carolina?"

He hitched one hip onto the corner of her desk. "So that's where the pretty accent comes from."

"Yes." His intense regard was making her palms sweat, so she cast about for another subject. "Why don't you...why don't you give me a little history of the company?" Maybe it wasn't as impersonal as she would have liked, but at least it was off the subject of *her* person.

Josh settled himself more comfortably on the edge of the desk. She tried not to stare at the long muscles of his thigh, but sheesh! the man was substantial.

"My dad built the business," Josh said. A little

smile played around his mouth, and she wondered if he'd noticed where her gaze had wandered. "I'm the youngest of four—all the rest girls. My sisters are married now and scattered between Montana and California. But growing up, Dad and I spent a lot of time at the construction sites—pure self-defense—because a houseful of women can be…daunting."

Hah. Lori didn't think this man could be daunted by anyone, but three sisters went a long way to explaining his self-deprecating charm. "Your father is retired now?"

Josh nodded. "He and Mom travel around in a Winnebago most of the year in order to serially spoil their ten grandchildren."

A big family. Sisters. Nieces and nephews. A wealth of people to turn to when times were bad.

"What about you?"

The sudden question made her jump. "M-me?"

"You." He smiled, that slow smile that turned her insides upside down. "Are you the petted youngest, the earnest eldest, what?"

"The lonely only." The words just slipped from her mouth and her face instantly heated. He didn't need to know anything about her. She didn't want a man, any man, to get that close.

It was as if he could read her mind. "Do I make you nervous?" he asked.

"Of course not."

His face softened, as if he knew she was lying but forgave her for it. "Well," he said. "You make *me* nervous."

She blinked. "I do?"

"Yeah." He let a beat go by. "It's not many women who flatten me."

Something warm flowed through the air between them. Lori felt it touch her skin, making it tingle, making her pulse skitter.

Her panic jumped to a new level. But this was a different kind of panic than she felt around most men. A new panic, or a forgotten one. Yet Josh was still dangerous.

She looked down at her notebook. "Perhaps we should get to work."

The warm current between them wasn't interrupted, but she knew he understood what she hadn't said. He rose to his feet. "Where did Lucy leave off?"

For the next half hour he took her around the office, explaining what Lucy hadn't had the chance to. Finally, they ended up in his office, where he showed her the rack of rolled blueprints that represented the company's current projects.

He settled into the big leather chair behind his desk and she perched on the chair opposite, her gaze snagging on plaques on the wall behind his head. Probably two dozen hung there, mostly team pictures of little kids. Boys, girls, basketball, baseball, football, their uniforms all proclaiming Anderson, Inc.

Josh twisted around to see what had caught her attention then turned back. "Now you know my secret."

"Your secret?" She didn't want to know it. Of course she did. "What secret?"

"I'm a sucker for a kid in a uniform." He sighed. "Any uniform."

She felt the smile start at her toes. When it reached her mouth, he smiled back, as if delighted. "Any uniform?" she asked.

He nodded sadly. "There's the cutest little Brownie who lives next door to me. I bought out her whole troop's worth of cookies." There was a gleaming wooden credenza behind him and he pulled open one of its drawers to display box after box of Girl Scout cookies. "I couldn't help myself."

His eyes were serious as they met hers. "So the next time you're in the mood for a thin mint, do me a favor, will you, and eat a whole box?" Then he grinned.

That heated, tingly current rushed like a flash flood toward her. It wasn't what she wanted, it wasn't what she was looking for, *not in the least,* but she didn't seem to have any choice but to let the feeling sweep over her. Sweep around her.

After two confusing years of marriage and three years during which she'd been both frozen and afraid, it was as if her feminine senses had come awake with one quick jolt. Or with one quick fall to the floor of the gym.

"Lori—" he started, then the phone rang. She jumped for it, but he held her off with his hand and lifted the receiver himself. She could feel his eyes on her, even as he spoke some important-sounding specifications.

Half embarrassed and half scared of what Josh

might be seeing on her face, Lori looked away. Her gaze moved to the Girl Scout cookies in the drawer to another photo, this one sitting on top of the credenza itself. It was a framed photo of a blond bride.

Josh's wife.

She didn't question her immediate conclusion. He certainly wouldn't choose to display just one of his sisters, and the beautiful woman looked like the type big, dark Josh would love.

He was married.

A feeling twisted her insides. Relief, she guessed. Whatever current she'd been feeling was imagined, or at the very worst, all on her side.

Josh was a married man. As he completed his phone call, she let that knowledge sink in. He wasn't any kind of threat to her. She didn't have to worry about him getting too close.

He was a husband.

At the click of receiver to cradle she looked up. Stood up. "I'll just get back to my desk."

His eyes narrowed. "Are you all right?"

Lori realized he wasn't wearing a ring. But for a man who worked with his hands, that was probably a good idea.

"Are you all right?" he asked again.

Of course. *Now* she was. Whatever was between them was something she'd obviously misread—she was so good at misreading men—and—

"What are you looking at?"

Until that moment, she hadn't realized she was looking at anything. But then he swung around to follow her gaze. They both stared at the photo of the bride.

Lori swallowed. ''Your wife?'' She thought her voice sounded normal.

Josh nodded.

''She's beautiful,'' Lori said. Then she smiled at him, because it was going to be okay. He was safe now. He was married.

But he didn't smile back as a shadow crossed his face. ''She was. Kay died five years ago. I'm a widower.''

Chapter Two

"I'm sorry for your loss," Lori said, her voice soft and sincere.

"Thank you." Josh looked away from the photo and back at the beautiful woman standing on the other side of his desk, cursing whatever it was about her that made him feel as if his hands, his feet, his Adam's apple were all too big. But he felt more than just physically awkward at the moment.

When was the last time he'd told someone he was a widower? In the small town of Whitehorn, after that first, awful day, everyone had known.

He cleared his throat.

She shuffled her feet.

"Is there—"

"Why don't—"

They both broke off.

Josh took a breath. "Ladies first."

Lori clutched her notebook against her chest. "I was going to ask if there was anything else you wanted to tell me before I went back to my desk."

Yeah. He wanted to tell her she was the most gorgeous woman he'd ever seen. It was the damn truth. Dark hair, blue eyes, creamy skin tinged with just a hint of peach. And her voice…it was moonlight. It was Southern, moonlit nights with fluttering lace curtains and bodies tangled on a bed.

He wanted to tell her he'd never considered himself a romantic man, but looking at her filled his thoughts with an embarrassment of bad lyrics to a country western song.

He wanted to tell her he'd fallen to the floor of the gym on Christmas Eve a settled, thirty-seven-year-old man and gotten up a randy teenager again, in instant lust for her long legs, her long dark hair, her full mouth. The way she'd stared back at him, her gaze filled with equal parts attraction and wariness, had done nothing to cool him off. That same gaze from her now didn't dampen his interest one bit.

Yet, see, there was that wariness, so instead he said, "Sit down for another minute. I want to know a little more about you."

Snails moved more quickly. Rain clouds appeared cheerier. After she finally returned to her chair, she reached inside her notebook and slid out a sheet of paper. "My resumé," she said, handing it to him.

He didn't even glance at it. "Why don't you tell me?"

She delivered the facts without emotion. "I moved to Montana from South Carolina last week. I signed on with the Whitehorn Temporary Agency. They sent me to Lucy. Lucy hired me."

Despite the dryness of the details, he could listen to that soft accent all day. South Carolina. Montana. The words were prettier in her Southern voice. "But why?" he asked. "Why Montana?"

She shrugged. "I grew up in the South. It was...time for something different. Someplace different."

"But why would you pick Whitehorn? We're not exactly Billings or Missoula."

She shrugged again, and her gaze dropped to her notebook.

Frustrated, he looked down at her resumé. She was twenty-eight years old. She'd gone to college in South Carolina, in a town he thought he recognized as located at the southern end of the state. She had a degree in business administration. He looked up. "You have a college degree and you're temping as a receptionist?"

"It's work," she said. "Experience."

That non-explanation sent him back to perusing her resumé. Which made her even more of a mystery. For more than two years following her college graduation, there was no employment listed. And in the past three years she'd held seven different jobs in several different South Carolina cities.

She was either easily bored or on the run.

He frowned. "Why—"

"Does it matter?" she interrupted. Steel suddenly hardened that soft Southern accent. "I'm technically employed by the temp agency, Mr. Anderson. They were satisfied. If you're not..." She shrugged, as if she wouldn't care if their paths never crossed again. "Call them and they'll send someone else over."

Okay. That put him in his place. Josh had no reason to feel she'd slapped him across the face, because she was right. Her employment history—or lack thereof—was none of his business. Not as long as she fulfilled her duties as Anderson, Inc.'s receptionist.

But he was irritated by her reticence because he wanted to know about her. Know her. And a few minutes ago he could have sworn there were sparks flying between them. Even before that, at the gym, her gaze meeting his had given him an I'm-Adam-you're-Eve rush that he hadn't felt in a long, long while.

With a mental shrug, he threw off his disappointment. Lori was beautiful, but so were a lot of women. She was an enigma, but he'd never been very good at puzzles. And the bottom line was that she wasn't interested in his...interest.

Sure, their mutual attraction was undeniable. Some things a man just knew; like, he knew which side to part his hair on or the exact spot to hit the basketball backboard for his best lay-up. But, right now Lori was putting up a sign that screamed Back Off in big neon letters, and she didn't need to flash it at him more than once.

So fine. The lady wanted nothing to do with him. He got it. He'd put his focus strictly on business and forget all about her.

He did okay for a while. A few hours. There were a dozen phone calls to field, a fire or two to put out at one of the construction sites. By afternoon, though, when he was back at his desk and staring at piles of work, the only thing moving through his head was the enticing, peachy scent of his new receptionist.

Ms. Hanson. He'd decided to call her that.

She responded in the prim manner of the school-mistress who had once ruled over this old building. With an efficiency that put his teeth on edge, she located the files he asked for. Tracked down a wayward bill. Watered the plant in the corner of his office that he usually treated to desert rations. After those words over her resumé, never once did she seem to be aware of him the way he couldn't help being aware of her.

When the sky outside his window started to darken, he wandered into the office's reception area to check on the supply of firewood in the brass box sitting beside the woodburning stove. But it was chock-full and there was a telltale, winter-air pink on the receptionist's cheeks and nose.

He frowned at her. "Ms. Hanson. Restocking the wood isn't your responsibility."

From the chair at her desk, she looked up at him. A pencil was stuck behind her ear, pushing a lock of hair forward so that it tangled in her curly black eye-lashes. "I don't mind."

"Well I do." His voice was just short of surly. "It's heavy. You could be hurt."

She brushed the hair out of her eyes. "I'm stronger than I look."

"So you've told me before," he said. "That day at the gym."

Her eyebrows rose. "Then you should believe me."

Instead of a good comeback the only thing that occurred to him was the memory of his body lying across hers, so he stomped back to his office and dropped behind his desk. He was acting like an oaf, or worse, a jerk, but there was something about her that aroused his protective instincts. It was that wariness. It was that Southern voice.

It was that peachy scent.

He opened up the nearest file and pretended he was looking at it. Perhaps he'd been all wrong about the mutual attraction. He was thirty-seven, supposedly old enough to know when something was there and when something wasn't. But maybe he was going through some pre-midlife crisis. Maybe he was entering some delusional psychological state in which he imagined beautiful women had the hots for him.

What a depressing thought.

Depressing enough to send him stomping back to the reception area. "Ms. Hanson?" he barked.

She blinked those astonishing blue eyes of hers. "Mr. Anderson?"

He hesitated. For God's sake, he couldn't come right out and ask her if she was attracted to him. There was probably some sort of employment code about that, not to mention what his sisters would say if they ever heard about it. His ears burned just imagining his mother's reaction to something so bad-mannered.

"Call me Josh," he muttered, then stalked back to his desk.

As the afternoon wore on, his mood darkened. Lori Hanson was hell on his ego. On Christmas Eve, he'd been forced into buying the first round of beers for the team because he'd been bested by a woman. He'd laughed about it, been a good sport about his friends' ribbing, because he had no problem with strong females. Risk-taking women were trouble, but not strong ones. Until he'd turned ten and outstripped all three of his older sisters in size, they'd flattened him often enough for him to be used to it.

But to make him doubt his powers of perception! That ability to recognize when a woman liked a man and when she didn't was the only thing a man had between himself and humiliation. Since Kay's death he'd enjoyed the companionship of women on occasion, always with the certainty that his attention was welcome. *Because he knew which women welcomed him.* Always.

But now…

Now he didn't know if he had his signals crossed or if the ones she sent out were the problem.

Sighing, he cast a look at the deepening dark outside his window, then at the clock. It was 4:55. Well, the good news was that any second now Ms. How-the-hell-do-I-know-what-she's-thinking Hanson would be on her way home. Then he could settle down and finish all the work that he should have been finishing that afternoon.

At 5:05 she hadn't left her desk.

At 5:20, the only movements she'd made were to run her hands through her hair and frown at the computer screen.

When it was exactly 5:30, he made himself exit his office and tell her she'd been free to leave for half an hour. She *hmm*ed absently, wrapped up with some paperwork on her desk.

By 5:45, he considered taking all *his* paperwork and dumping it on her, because only one of them seemed to be able to work in the other's presence.

At 6:00 he couldn't take it anymore. "Ms. Hanson," he yelled from his desk.

"Yes, Mr. Anderson?" came from the reception area.

"*Josh.*" He grabbed hold of his temper. "Ms. Hanson, it's time for you to go home."

He thought she made another one of those absent *hmm*s. With a look at the massive amount of work he had yet to finish, he strode into the reception area. "Ms. Hanson," he said from between his teeth. "Go home."

She didn't look at him. "Soon."

"You've done enough for today." *While I've done*

nothing but make myself crazy. "It's time to knock off."

She sucked in one edge of her bottom lip. "I'll leave when you do."

Staring at her mouth, he knew if she stayed he'd never get *anything* done. Obviously, someone had sent her here to drive him over the edge. One of his competitors. One of his so-called friends. His sister Dana, who had never truly forgiven him for catching her entire Senior Prom date on audiotape.

God, now his delusional thoughts were sliding into paranoia. Exasperated, his voice came out strangled. "Ms. Hanson, what the hell is wrong with you? I tell you to go home and you stay. What is it—are you afraid of the dark?"

She stilled. Her eyelashes lifted to reveal those blue-as-some-exotic-flower eyes.

Josh's gut twisted. *Don't,* he thought, suddenly as desperate not to know any more about her as he'd been desperate to know more about her earlier. *Don't say it.*

But then she did. "Yes."

Lori knew Josh wasn't happy as he held open Anderson Inc.'s front door for her. "You should have said something," he grumbled, following her into the darkness.

She pretended the heat on her cheeks was from the cold night air, not her embarrassment. "I'm sorry. It's just that I'm in a new place...it's unfamiliar—"

"Don't apologize," he said shortly. "I should have thought of it myself."

It wasn't *his* fault. "It's me. The dark parking lot…"

"I'm going to get one of the men to install a light out there tomorrow," he said.

Halting on the brick walkway, she turned to him. "Oh, no—"

"Lori." In the darkness, his body was a massive shadow, but his voice was gentle. "It's done. But to ease your mind even more, remember this isn't the big city. You're in Whitehorn now."

"Yes." Looking up, she took a deep breath of the clean, icy air. Whitehorn, Montana. "The stars seem so clear, so close here," she said. "It's as if someone polished the sky."

"Someone did," he answered lightly. "We like things to look their best when Southern girls arrive."

She laughed. "Well, I'm impressed. I didn't expect it to be quite so beautiful." With a hand, she gestured toward the building they'd exited. "I didn't expect a construction company office to look like an old schoolhouse either."

Josh started toward the parking lot again. "It *is* an old schoolhouse. Miss Lilah Anderson's schoolhouse, as a matter of fact. Dad and I rescued it a few years ago."

"Lilah Anderson? A relation?"

"Yep. An aunt. I forget how many greats," Josh answered. "My sister Dana knows, though, she's the genealogist in the family."

"Your roots go deep in Whitehorn, then." Lori had roots here too, roots that she wanted to reconnect to. Roots that she hoped would help her build a new life. "It must be nice."

"Are you rootless, Lori?"

She figured he was thinking of her resumé and the many jobs she'd had and cities she'd lived in over the past years. But she didn't want to go into that. "I don't have a big family like you do," she said instead. "My mother died when I was twenty-three, after a long illness. We were...alone in the world."

And how alone she'd felt during her mother's illness. So alone that she'd made a mistake she'd been paying for every day since.

They reached her car. Though Lori had her keys in her hand, Josh leaned against the driver's-side door, blocking her way. Goodness. His shoulders had to be twice the size of the average man's.

"You make me realize I shouldn't take so much for granted," he said. "My family's always been there for me. And the business was always there for me, too."

Lori dipped her hands in the pocket of her coat. "So you always wanted the business? You always wanted to build things?" She could see him, she thought, a tall gangly kid following his father around with a hammer and a hundred questions.

His grin sliced whitely through the darkness. "I wanted to be a cowboy until I was nine years old and I fell off my friend's horse and onto my keister. Then good ol' Smokey stomped all over my hand. Couldn't sit down or make a fist for a week.''

"Poor baby." Lori shook her head, amused by the picture he painted. "Though you're ruining Montana's image for me. I thought all western men were horsemen.''

"Yeah," he said dryly. "Just like we all smoke Marlboros and drag our Christmas trees behind sleighs through snowy fields."

"Wearing ten-gallon hats," she added.

"And sheepskin jackets."

She couldn't help but smile. "You don't have a sheepskin jacket? I think I'm going to cry."

"I'll get one tomorrow," he said promptly. "Just so you won't."

The teasing note in his voice made her nervous again. "Well…" she started.

"Well?"

"I guess it's time for me to take myself and my fractured preconceptions home." She drew her hand and her car keys from her pocket.

He moved away from the door so she could unlock it. "It's not that I don't like horses, Lori. Just that I like them best when they're standing and I'm standing too."

When she opened the door, the car's overhead light pooled on Josh's heavy construction boots but didn't come close to illuminating his face, somewhere above her. "You seem to have bad luck with things falling on you," she said, daring to tease a little about their meeting in the gym.

"I wouldn't say it's bad luck at all."

With just those words, her pulse quickened again. She looked up at him, then swallowed, because he was so big and because there was that current running between them, that hot, tingly current she'd worked so hard to ignore all day. She had no business feeling this. For Josh, or for any man. It was too easy for her to become dependent on one. The wrong one.

"Josh." She meant to say the word as a warning, but instead it came out uncertain.

"Lori." He took a step closer, and she automatically shrank against the car. He froze. He muttered to himself. He turned away from her. "Good night."

"Good night."

But before she had the door shut, he turned back. "Lori."

"Yes?"

His face was still in shadow, but it didn't take night vision for her to know he was battling himself. "Are you…is there…" He broke off, muttering again.

"What do you want, Josh?"

His voice was rueful. "For the moment, the answer to a question."

"Yes?"

He sighed. "Did you come to Whitehorn to be with someone?"

To be with a man, he meant. "No, Josh." Lori almost laughed. "Good night." Shutting the car door, she wondered what he'd think if she told him she'd come to Whitehorn for precisely the opposite reason. She was here to get away from someone.

To get away from a man.

Chapter Three

Before work a few mornings later, Josh sat on a weight bench at the gym, pushing himself through another set of bicep curls. Sweat ran down his neck and glistened on his arms. He worked his muscles to the failure point, knowing that he wouldn't make it through the day without burning off some of his restless energy.

Dealing with Lori Hanson wasn't getting any easier. She continued to be a distracting, enigmatic presence in his office. He still didn't know if he had his signals crossed or if she sent out hot and cold messages on purpose.

Though he'd been spending a lot of time out of the office, he still made it back by five o'clock every day to walk her to her car. As he'd promised, the parking lot was brightly lit now, but he felt better seeing her off himself.

Someone dropped to the bench beside him. Josh kept pumping the weights, thinking about how Lori had looked beneath the new light the night before, her nose pinking with the cold, her dark hair curling against her cheek. He'd had to hold himself back from placing his palm there. Worse, he'd yet to shake the feeling that part of her wanted him to do that very thing.

"Hell, Josh," said a familiar voice. "I said 'good morning' and I've been sitting here for five minutes waiting for a response, but you haven't done anything but grunt and sweat."

Jerked from his reverie, Josh turned his head. "Oh. Andy. Hey." He'd known Andy McKenna for a dozen years.

Andy picked up a couple of nearby dumbbells and started his own set of curls. "What's eating you?"

Josh let his weights slip to the floor. His arm muscles burned. "The usual."

Andy looked over. "A work problem?"

"Woman problem."

Thud-thud. Andy's weights dropped. So did his jaw. "You're kidding, right?"

"Why would you say that?" Josh asked.

"Because, buddy, you haven't let yourself have a woman problem, not once, in the last five years."

Since Kay's death, Andy meant. Josh shifted on the bench, stretching out his legs to inspect the laces of his cross-trainers. It was true. He hadn't felt the need for anything more than the most casual relationships with women since then. Nothing heavy enough to be classified a problem. He grunted. "I have one now."

"Well, hallelujah," Andy said. "Good ol' Josh has a woman problem."

Josh shot the other man a look. "Gee, thanks."

He grinned. "Misery loves company and all that. So tell Dear Andy the problem. Is the lady married? Does she have a boyfriend?"

"No." As he'd walked her to her car that first night, Josh had wondered that himself. But she'd said she hadn't come to Whitehorn to be with a man. He ran a hand over his damp hair. "Andy, you know when a woman's interested, right?"

"Hmm." The other man reached for the dumbbells he'd dropped. "Well, I've made my share of blunders over the years, but I'd say that now I'm pretty good at distinguishing between a smile and a, well, *smile.*"

"And how old are you?" Josh asked.

"Thirty-five."

Younger than Josh, which meant he couldn't rule out that pre-midlife crisis condition.

"Geez, Josh." Andy stopped lifting again. "You look serious. What the hell's the matter?"

Josh shook his head. "I—"

Andy's low whistle interrupted him. "Wow. Would you look at that." With his chin, he gestured toward the glass wall in front of them, the wall through which they could see the basketball courts and the running track surrounding them.

A woman was stretching in the far lane of one

curve. "'That,'" said Josh. "Is precisely my problem. Lori Hanson, my temporary receptionist."

"Oh, buddy." Andy gazed on him with pity. "I don't blame you. She looks like trouble." He switched his gaze back to the track, where Lori was now starting her run. "Uh-oh. Wouldn't you know it, Wily Rick Weber is on the scent."

Ahead of Lori on the track, a lean, curly-haired man paused and bent over, as if his shoe needed retying. It was only too obvious to Josh that the other runner had noticed Lori and was waiting for her to catch up to him.

Andy snorted. "Is he always the first to sniff out new prey, or what?"

Josh lifted the hem of his T-shirt to wipe the sweat out of his eyes, then leaned forward. How would Lori respond to the ever-charming Wily Rick?

She didn't.

Even though Rick timed it so that he started jogging again just as Lori reached him, even though he smiled whitely, oozing friendliness that Josh could feel even through the plate glass, Lori didn't even glance at the other man. As a matter of fact, she picked up her pace, causing Wily to have to leap forward in order to keep up with her.

His mouth moved. Probably saying something witty, Josh thought. Something far more interesting than "Ms. Hanson, find me the Feeney file, please." But she responded to Rick with even fewer syllables and less animation that she did when Josh spoke.

Surprise crossed Rick's oh-so-slick and handsome

face, and he slowed a bit, letting Lori get ahead. Strike one for Wily.

"Well," Andy said. "Rick hasn't bowled her over."

"Neither have I," Josh muttered.

And just like Josh himself, Rick didn't find it easy to give up on Lori either. As Josh watched, the other man caught up with her again and tried to start another conversation. Her slight grimace made clear, to Josh anyway, that she didn't appreciate Wily's second attempt.

Josh stood up. "I'm going to take a few laps myself," he told Andy.

The other man's grin was knowing. "You do that. But be careful. I haven't seen you chasing—I mean *running*—in a long time, old friend."

Josh didn't look back. He wasn't chasing. He was going after Lori to make sure Wily wasn't annoying her, not because of the apparently one-sided attraction he had for her. That attraction he was determined to put a lid on, because it would be hell on his brain and his business if it was allowed to simmer unchecked for the remainder of Lucy's maternity leave.

Just as Josh jogged onto the track, Wily jogged off, a look of baffled disappointment on his face. He didn't even acknowledge Josh's two-fingered salute. It wasn't often Rick struck out, and it looked as if it was going to take him some time to recover.

Josh was smiling when he caught up with Lori. He brushed off the niggling notion that his entire reason for joining her was now heading for the men's show-ers. "Good morning," he said.

She looked over at him, her eyes widening, then she trained her gaze back on the track in front of her. "Good morning, Mr. Anderson."

"Josh."

She made another of those maddening, absent *hmm*s that she liked to torture him with.

"Well. How are you this morning?"

"Fine." She didn't look at him.

"I, um, thought I'd let you know that I'm stopping off at the Feeney site before I come into the office this morning."

"All right."

When he thought about it, maybe he should still bring up Rick and his attempts at flirtation. He hesi-tated, then plunged in, unable to come up with some way to ease into the subject. "I saw Rick talking to you," he said.

"Who?"

"Wil—Rick Weber. The curly-haired guy who was running with you."

"Oh. Him."

The little breeze they generated running caused her peach scent to waft enticingly over Josh's face. He tried not breathing through his nose. "He's okay, but he has a reputation for two-timing."

Now she looked at him, her expression bewildered. "Why would you tell me that?"

So I could feel my feet grow five sizes larger, Josh thought. But he went on doggedly. "I just thought you should know because…I, well… Well, he was hitting on you.''

''I'm not interested in him.''

''Good.'' She shot him a look, and he hoped he didn't look as satisfied as he felt. To cover it up, he cleared his throat and then forced himself to test the waters again. ''But just in case you *are* interested in dating, I do know a few good men I could introduce you to.''

Did he imagine it, or was her face turning a shade of red that bespoke embarrassment, not exertion?

''I didn't come to Whitehorn to meet men.''

''I didn't say that you did,'' Josh answered, plodding on with his offer. ''But you're a young woman. Certainly you'd like a social life. I have friends who—''

She shook her head. ''Please, Josh. I don't want to meet anybody. Please.''

The tone in her voice was urgent. Anxious.

Despite her discomfort, he had to admit he felt that satisfaction again. ''Okay. Sure. No problem,'' he answered.

''Josh.'' She abruptly stopped running and he skidded to a halt beside her.

''What?'' he asked.

Her chest moved up and down, her breaths still coming fast. Josh tried not to stare, focusing instead on her dark eyelashes that hid the expression in her eyes.

''I'd even be grateful,'' she said, ''if you'd…pass the word around the gym.''

Josh blinked at her. "Pass what word?"

Her shoulders hunched in an embarrassed sort of shrug. "I've...sworn off men for the moment, okay? I'm not eager to meet any, date any, become entangled with any." She darted one swift look at him. "With anyone, no matter how...appealing."

With him, she meant.

Then she dashed off in the direction of the women's locker room, leaving Josh staring after her. Well, he thought. Finally, there was his answer. It wasn't mixed signals. It wasn't him misreading. It wasn't that she didn't feel the same attraction he did—she'd even implied she found him appealing. But the fact was, she'd sworn off men.

He could understand that. Appreciate it. Abide by it. For God's sake, he hadn't paid any but the most cursory attention to his own social life in the last five years.

And *why* she'd sworn off men was none of his business either.

Josh showered and dressed quickly, telling himself he was glad to have the Lori problem straightened out. It meant he could refocus his attention on business. That he could smother the attraction he felt for her because she wanted to smother it too.

He even managed a cheerful goodbye to the kid who manned the check-in desk as he left. Even when he encountered Lori at the door leading outside, his lightened mood didn't change. Much.

He smiled at her as he held open the door. "I'll be

in around ten. You can get me on my cell phone, though.''

''The Feeney site,'' she replied, stepping onto the concrete sidewalk, her gym bag in one hand.

The morning had grown colder in the hour he'd been working out. Lori's second step found a patch of ice that had been a shallow puddle sixty minutes before. The sole of her shoe lost purchase, and Josh saw her heel slide out from under her.

Her free arm windmilled.

Without a second thought, a first, any thought at all, he reached out, sliding his arm around her waist. With a jerk, he swept her upright and against him.

She screamed.

Startled, Josh's arm tightened. It wasn't a shriek of surprise, or an I'm-about-to-fall squeal. It was—

She screamed again, fighting wildly against his arm.

Startled again, he let her go.

She whirled to face him, her face white, her eyes huge pools of blue fear.

Fear.

He remembered her reaction when he bumped into her on the running track Christmas Eve. He remembered her shrinking back against her car when he'd stepped close to her in the parking lot.

Her free hand lifted. ''I'm sorry,'' she said hoarsely. ''I'm sorry. I was…''

''Scared?'' he supplied.

Color rushed up from the collar of her coat to redden her cheeks. At least she didn't look like she was seeing a ghost anymore. "Yes. But thanks for not letting me fall."

"Anytime," Josh replied. He wasn't surprised when she hurried away from him, in the direction of her car. "Anytime," he said again, staring after her retreating figure.

Of course, the next time he probably *would* let Lori fall. Because he couldn't bear to frighten her again. And touching would. Getting close to her would. He was certain of that.

Because there was a terrible, sick feeling in his gut that told him exactly why Lori Hanson had sworn off men.

Lori bustled around the Anderson, Inc., office, grateful that Josh was stopping by the Feeney site before coming in. She needed the opportunity to recover her composure. She needed time to convince herself that right this minute Josh wasn't booking his skittish temporary receptionist a rubber room.

She needed to believe he wasn't aware that a man's touch—any man's touch—made her jump as if she'd been recently beaten.

Because that wasn't the case. Her ex-husband hadn't hit her in over two years.

Lori closed her eyes against those memories, thinking instead of Josh. As he'd saved her from falling, his big body had been warm against hers. He'd smelled of soap and cold Montana air. And though her heart had been pounding with its old, instinctive panic, there had been another feeling running counter to the fear. Feelings.

Interest. Curiosity. Excitement.

But that was just all the more confusing! She'd been honest with Josh when she'd said she'd sworn off men. Yet the truth was, when he'd brought up the idea of her socializing, of her *dating,* for a moment she'd wondered what it would be like to date *him.*

Of course, after her little panic attack outside the gym this morning, he probably couldn't imagine fixing her up with someone, let alone himself. But that was fine. That was what she wanted. She wanted to do a good job as his receptionist, nothing more.

By the time Josh arrived from the Feeney site, she had her emotions back under control. As the door shut behind him, she scooped up the pile of pink slips that were his messages.

"Good morning," she said, as if they hadn't already encountered one another that day. "Your messages, Mr. Anderson." She held them out.

He approached her desk. "Josh," he countered, though his voice was mild. "You're supposed to call me Josh." When his large hand slid the papers from hers, their fingers didn't touch.

She was glad. Though she'd promised herself to curb her jumpiness around him, her reactions weren't always easy to control. Her breath, for example. As he hesitated in front of her, she couldn't seem to catch her breath.

She swallowed, trying to meet his eyes without flushing. "Is...is everything okay?"

There was something different about Josh now, she noticed. His big body seemed stiller, calmer than before. Which only made her feel that much more gauche. "Did you want something?" she asked, when he didn't say anything.

"No." He smiled, that slow, wide, warm one that seemed to brighten the whole room. "Everything's fine now."

The rest of the morning echoed his words. For the first time they worked in an atmosphere of friendly harmony. He didn't bark out assignments, she didn't jump when he walked into the reception area. It was almost as if Josh had turned his personality on Low. While he couldn't do anything to mitigate his massive size, she thought he'd somehow banked his normal forcefulness.

Their business relationship might just work out.

At noon, she retrieved from the refrigerator a salad she'd made at home and carried it to her desk. Whistling softly, Josh walked out of his office, his coat caught on two fingers.

He glanced over at her. "I'm off to—" His mouth turned down in obvious distaste. "That's lunch?"

"Well, yes." Looking down, she couldn't stop from making her own face. When she'd made the salad that morning, the lettuce had already been half wilted. Now it looked like it had gone into a dead faint.

Josh shook his head. "Why don't you come with me? We'll find something better."

"Oh, no," she said instantly. Not when their business relationship was just getting established.

He hesitated. "C'mon, Lori. I know you said you didn't want me to introduce you to any men, and I respect that. But I know some other people you might like to meet."

"Oh, I couldn't." She drew her chair closer to the desk to make sure he got the message. "There's the phones, the business…"

"The machine will take the calls and this *is* business," he countered. "I'm going over to the Hip Hop Café to check the crew's progress. I told you about that project, right? We're rebuilding the restaurant after the arson fire last month. As the company's receptionist, you should know the kinds of things we do. I'm meeting the owner there, Melissa North. I'll introduce you. You'll like her."

Melissa North. Lori hoped her face didn't betray her sudden eagerness. Melissa North. She weighed the prospect of meeting Melissa North against the danger of spoiling this very newfound peace with Josh by spending more time in his company.

As if he sensed her mental struggle, Josh used his own weapon. He smiled, that easy, patient, warm one. "Let's go," he said, nodding toward the door. "It's business."

Because it was business, Lori didn't feel obligated to keep up a conversation on the short drive from the office to the heart of downtown Whitehorn. When Josh turned his big, black four-wheeler into a parking place, she was out of her seat and on the sidewalk before he had the emergency brake on. One business associate certainly didn't expect another business associate to open her door for her and help her out, despite the long leap to the ground.

Because it was business, she kept her attention strictly on the discussion between Josh and the Hip Hop site foreman as they toured the reconstruction. The restaurant had burnt to the ground a few weeks before and the Anderson crew was just beginning to rebuild.

Though she didn't understand all of the conversation, Lori was fascinated to learn that some time capsules had been found buried in the restaurant's original foundation. When Josh bent over to inspect the cavity where they'd been discovered, his thigh-length parka rode up. It might not have been completely businesslike of Lori to notice the long muscles of his hamstrings or the tautness of his gluteus maximus muscles beneath his worn jeans, but it was natural, right? She had an interest in fitness.

By the time Josh straightened, she was perusing a set of plans unrolled on the hood of the foreman's truck. All business.

Josh checked his watch. "Time to meet Melissa," he said.

Lori looked up. "She's not coming here?"

"We're meeting her at the counter of the Big Sky Five & Dime." His thumb jerked to the small variety store across the street. "She's probably waiting for us."

Lori's heart hammered as she crossed the street in

Josh's wake. Now that the moment had come, she wondered if she should have stayed safely back at her desk after all. Melissa North.

At the door of the Big Sky Five & Dime, Josh turned to watch Lori's reluctant progress. One of his eyebrows rose. "Something the matter?"

Taking a breath, she shook her head, then hurried her footsteps. Josh had witnessed enough of her craziness for one day. With a businesslike cloak, she'd hide from him her inner turmoil.

He held the door for her. "There's a counter and a couple of booths at the back that have gained new life since the Hip Hop went out of commission."

At a calm pace, Lori walked down the narrow aisles in the direction Josh indicated. Her gaze darted over the customers she encountered, though, her stomach clenching as she wondered if she would recognize Melissa.

As the smell of french fries and coffee grew stronger, Josh called from behind her, "Take a right." Lori obeyed, coming upon a counter with five stools and beyond that, two four-person booths upholstered in red vinyl.

In the nearest booth a couple sat side-by-side. The woman laughed, and her dark hair slid away from her cheek as she lifted her face for the man's brief kiss. Then he whispered something in her ear, and she turned her head toward Lori and Josh.

She looked beautiful, with fair skin and blue eyes. She looked happy and friendly.

She looked just as Lori had imagined her half sister might.

It was lucky that Josh stepped in to make the introductions, because Lori felt anything but businesslike as she met Melissa and Wyatt North. In seconds she was knee-to-knee with the other woman, though, as she and Josh took the seat on the other side of the booth.

Lori's tongue remained knotted, so it was lucky, too, that it took some minutes to order their lunch—Josh told her the only substantial food offered was grilled cheese sandwiches—and get the Hip Hop details out of the way. By the time her plate was in front of her, Lori had relaxed a little.

When the men started talking about the arson investigation, Melissa grinned at her. "Would you be horribly offended if I snitched a french fry?" she asked.

"Oh. Oh, no." Lori flushed and pushed the plate toward the center of the table. "I should have offered. Forgive me."

"Done." Melissa bit into the french fry with relish. "It's the only thing they make nearly as good as the Hip Hop."

Lori took up her own fry, but her stomach was too nervous to eat. "I'm sorry to hear about what happened to your restaurant."

Melissa shook her head. "Don't get me started. Half the time I want to cry and the other half I want to strangle whoever did such a destructive thing."

"They haven't caught who did it?"

"No." Melissa sighed, but then took another french fry and turned her attention to Lori. "So tell me about you."

"I…" This wasn't the time or place to blurt out the truth. Lori licked her lips. "I'm new to White-horn. As Josh said earlier, I'm his temporary recep-tionist."

"He's a good man," Melissa said, then her gaze sharpened. "But you know that, right?"

Lori bit into her french fry so she could nod instead of talking.

"Still, it can't be easy to settle someplace new," Melissa went on. "Did you have a special reason for coming to Whitehorn?"

Lori swallowed. "I wanted to set down some roots."

Melissa nodded, as if she understood. "I grew up in Whitehorn, and then my mother and I moved when I was a senior in high school. I spent the next few years mooning over Wyatt and doing what I had to come back." She cocked her head. "But it was com-ing home for me. How did you even hear about Whitehorn?"

"My mother told me about it. She was from White-horn."

One of Melissa's dark eyebrows rose. "From here? Who is she?"

Lori didn't think her mother's name would mean anything to Melissa. Her mother had said that Charlie Avery, Lori and Melissa's father, had been a philan-derer, and that her parents had moved the family out of state as soon as she'd discovered she was pregnant. "Jill Hanson. The daughter of Roy and Jane Hanson. But they're all gone now."

"Oh." Melissa's face softened "I'm sorry. That must be lonely sometimes." She reached out and covered Lori's hand with her own.

Lori froze. Women didn't send her into a panic, but she hadn't felt comfortable with *anyone's* touch in a long while. Because of the kind of marriage she'd had and the way she'd been on the move after it, she hadn't had the opportunity to develop any kind of relationship that involved touching, not even something as casual but as considerate as this.

She stared at their joined hands, at the similar skin tone, at Melissa's slender fingers that reminded her so much of her own. Tears burned the corners of her eyes.

"Lori?" Josh softly called her name.

Blinking, she turned her head toward his. Her breath caught. There was concern on his rugged, handsome face. Kindness.

Then something more. As she looked up at him, with her half sister Melissa's hand still covering hers, Lori felt her heart open up, and she saw Josh watch it happen.

Warmth, trust, promise. Like petals, the feelings tentatively unfurled in her chest, a blossom taking its chance on a winter sun.

Chapter Four

At one end of the weight room, Josh leaned against a Nautilus machine and pretended he was merely resting between sets instead of what he was really doing—resting between sets while watching Lori work out. It was a kickboxing class today, in the adjacent aerobics area. The class was unusually small, probably because it was New Year's Eve and most people had headed home early this Saturday afternoon to prepare for their evening celebrations.

But Billy Blanks and his Tae-Bo enthusiasts would be proud. Even without the communal energy of a full class, Lori's sidekicks punched outward with determined force.

Her jaw looked clenched in concentration. The tendrils of hair that had escaped her ponytail hung in

damp question marks against her cheeks. In a baggy
pair of sweatpants cut off at the knees and an over-
sized T-shirt, she should have looked tough. Com-
petent.

She did. But why she worked so hard on that
strength clawed at him.

Her terrified reaction when he'd stopped her from
falling a few mornings ago, added to her self-defense
attack when he'd bumped into her on the running
track the first day they'd met could equal only one
thing. A man had hurt her. Not just emotionally, but
physically too.

The certainty made him sick. And relieved, though
that sounded more warped than it should. He wasn't
happy about whatever experiences she'd endured, of
course, but he was glad to finally understand her skit-
tishness. He was damn glad to know so that he could
quit adding to her disquiet with his attempts at flirtation.

None of this changed her appeal for him, though.
God, no. Now she was more than beautiful. In every
bead of sweat, in every kick, in every lap, he read
Lori's determination never to be a victim again. He
admired that.

But overlying his regard for her tenacious guts and
her uncommon gorgeousness was something that sent
him running. Tenderness. Protectiveness.

He didn't want to feel that way.

So he reminded himself that she needed healing,
not him. She wasn't in the market for a fling any more

than he was. Neither one of them was in any emotional place to want anything more.

As Josh watched, Lori changed direction, back-kicking for all she was worth. If only he could kick off his raging guard-dog complex as easily. Such an ability would come in handy right this minute, Josh thought, as he spied Wily Rick Weber sauntering through the weight room, his gaze glued on Lori.

Josh suppressed a feral growl, instead smiling at the other man as he intercepted Rick's straight path toward the aerobics room. "Hey there, Rick."

It took Wily a moment to switch his focus to Josh. "Anderson," he said absently, already moving forward to brush by him. Then Wily paused, the expression on his face reflecting his crafty nickname. "Wait a minute," he said softly. "She works for you, doesn't she?"

Josh folded his arms across his chest and looked down at the smaller man. "Who?"

Wily's eyes narrowed. "Yeah, right. As if you don't know who I mean. Her name's Lori, correct?"

No one ever said Wily was dumb, just trouble. "Mmm," Josh answered, shrugging.

Wily's eyes squeezed to suspicious slits. "Don't try scaring me off, Josh. There's no reason I shouldn't ask her out. It's not like *you* have a claim."

"What the hell do you mean by that?" The hair on the back of Josh's neck bristled.

Wily gave him a smarmy guy-to-guy smile. "Word is you're more monk than man, Anderson. Can't see you trying to melt the ice queen over there as your first foray into romance after all these years.'' His smile widened. ''Leave the hard ones to me, big guy.''

Smarmy, wily, stinkin' Rick Weber had just insulted him. Lifted Josh's ego and dumped it on its head. He was so pissed, he just stared at the jerk.

Which apparently gave Rick the idea that he was letting him get away with it, because Rick smiled again. ''I've suddenly found myself dateless for the New Year's party at the country club tonight. Watch this. Give me five minutes and I'll make her say 'yes.''' He swaggered forward.

Until Josh grabbed his arm and hauled him back. ''No,'' he said.

Wily frowned. ''No?''

''No.'' Josh would have let his ego take the beating, but he couldn't let Rick Give-me-five-minutes Weber try to make Lori do anything. ''She's busy tonight.'' Hadn't Lori asked him herself to put out the word around the gym that she was off-limits?

Rick's eyebrows rose. ''Maybe I'll make certain of that myself. Maybe I'll just show up at her place tonight and hope she invites me in for…something.''

Josh squeezed Rick's arm, the idea of him on Lori's doorstep tightening a sudden knot in his belly. ''She's already going out with me.''

''Oh, yeah?'' Rick asked. ''Where?''

''The country club.'' Josh didn't have time to come up with something else. He *had* been going to the country club celebration. Stag.

''Hmm.'' Rick's face turned down in a considering

frown. Finally, he shrugged. "I'll see you there, then." Shaking off Josh's hand, he sauntered in the other direction, toward the men's locker room, leaving Josh to face Lori, who didn't know she'd just gotten herself a New Year's Eve date.

Her class over, Lori walked out of the aerobics room, blotting her face with the end of the towel hanging around her neck. When she saw him, she halted, a shy smile on her face. "Josh."

Oh, he felt like a heel. In the past few days, since figuring out what made her afraid, he'd been so damn careful with her. He'd given her space. He'd made sure he never showed how he gulped back his lust when she walked into his office, her peachy scent preceding her. Her ease with him had grown by leaps and bounds and now, damn it, the leaps were going to be backward ones.

"Lori, good to see you." He cleared his throat, keenly aware that asking her out was going to put her guard back up. "Do you, uh, do you have any New Year's Eve plans?"

A shadow darkened her jewel-blue eyes. "No."

"I was hoping…I was wondering…I'm going to the Whitehorn Country Club tonight for a dinner dance." His feet, his hands, his Adam's apple felt as if they were growing like Pinocchio's nose. Damn, she made him that edgy, even when he was asking her out for her own good.

She frowned and took a small step back. "Josh, I—"

"The Norths are going to be there," he said hastily,

thinking of Rick's smarmy smile and his notion to
show up on Lori's doorstep. "Melissa and Wyatt.
Some other people I think you'll like, too."

"Melissa?" Lori swallowed. "The Norths?"

Josh nodded, pleased that mentioning the other
couple seemed to pique her interest. He knew she'd
established an instant rapport with Melissa when
they'd met. "We've planned to sit together."

"I'd…"

Josh marshalled his thoughts, trying to come up
with some additional enticements.

"…like that."

"You would?" He stared at her, trying to squelch
the heated rush of satisfaction pulsing through him.
This wasn't a date, he reminded himself. This was a
rescue. That's all.

Not a date, a rescue. He was still trying to tell
himself that as he escorted Lori into the Whitehorn
Country Club a few hours later. If it were a date, he
would have allowed himself to comment on the
beauty of her shoulders, their delicate strength revealed by the off-the-shoulder black velvet of her
dress. If it were a date, he would have told her he
liked the sophisticated twist of her hair on the back
of her head. If it were a date, he would have touched
her elbow, the small of her back, as he led her toward
their table.

And if it were a date, he wouldn't be in such a
damn lousy mood because he'd have been able to do
all those things…and more. Instead, he was her self-

appointed, self-sacrificing watchdog, destined to spend the evening looking, smelling, but not touching. Never touching. *Grrr.*

Lucky for him, the other couples at their round, ten-person table were in much better moods than he. Melissa instantly caught Josh's unspoken signal and insisted Lori sit on her right. Josh tipped the chair beside Lori's against the tabletop to indicate it was taken, then headed to the bar. He took a big swallow of his whiskey on his way back and set Lori's chardonnay in front of her before dropping into his seat.

She looked away from Melissa and smiled at him. "Thanks, Josh. The next round is on me."

He waved her thanks away, but his mood lightened at the sparkle in her sapphire eyes. She turned back to her conversation with Melissa and Josh half-closed his lids, savoring his drink and the animated chatter of the two women.

He could do this, he thought. He could ignore the persistent tug of his hormones, the ones that kept clamoring for him to get closer to her, to touch her, to treat her like a real date. The nice-guy thing came naturally to him—probably because he'd grown up with three older sisters who were never shy about sharing with him the kind of stupid things men could do.

So he was going to be the nice guy. The smart guy who didn't push for something Lori didn't want.

The evening progressed smoothly enough. The five-course dinner was excellent, despite Melissa's adamant assertion that the Hip Hop served better roast

beef and roast potatoes, not to mention chocolate
mousse. Of course another of their tablemates, Darcy
Montague, waitress at the Hip Hop and now fiancée
of Whitehorn detective Mark Kincaid, loyally agreed.

The Norths, Darcy and Mark, and the other friends
at the table listened avidly, however, when Lori mentioned the traditional Southern dishes she'd grown up
with. Despite the fact that everyone said they were
stuffed, to the last person they all sighed over her
description of a bourbon-laced bread pudding.

Then the plates were cleared away and the dancing
started. A swing band struck up a Glenn Miller favorite, and within seconds their table was deserted as
couples streamed toward the dance floor.

Dancing. Josh hadn't thought about that.

Lori turned toward him, her smile bright, her
cheeks flushed. "Thank you again for inviting me,"
she said. "Your friends are so welcoming." With the
table's candlelight gleaming off her half-bared shoulders, her pale skin held the lustre of pearls.

If this were a date, he would have gone poker-hard
with lust.

But it was a rescue, so he shifted on his chair and
tried to appear relaxed. He would have given his best
backhoe to take her in his arms on the dance floor,
but he knew wary Lori wouldn't welcome the offer.
If her heart pounded against his, it would be in the
jerky rhythm of a spooked jackrabbit, not the speeding beat of an aroused woman.

But she didn't know *he* knew that. Her gaze darted
toward the dancers, then back at him, and he could

see the wheels starting to turn in her mind. She scooted a little away, her worry written all over her face.

He leaned forward as if to share a secret. "I hope you don't mind if I don't ask you to dance."

"Oh…well…"

"I'm a lousy dancer," he went on. "It's the big feet, you know. I avoid the activity whenever possible."

The tension slid right out of her. Her smile looked relieved. "I don't mind at all. We'll just sit here and talk. How's that?"

"Perfect." He tossed back the dregs of his whiskey. "Tell me some more about the South."

She did. As the occupants of their table came and went, sometimes dancing and sometimes resting, Lori focused her attention on Josh. In words spoken in that smooth Southern accent of hers, she drew pictures of the place where she'd grown up, pictures of a childhood eating something called Frogmore stew under Spanish-moss-draped oaks, with friends who took their cast nets out on weekends to go crabbing in the nearby estuary-fed creeks.

Fascinated by these glimpses of a different world, fascinated by the way her lush mouth moved and the way her eyes laughed when he did, Josh forgot where he was.

He forgot that he was supposed to be rescuing Lori, not reacting like a normal, red-blooded man to her beauty.

Until Wyatt dropped into his chair and pleaded

with Melissa for mercy. "Honey, it's not long until midnight. You need to give me a breather if I'm going to lay on you the best New Year's kiss of your life."

Hell, Josh thought. Midnight. Kisses. He'd planned that he and Lori would be well on their way home before midnight to avoid all that.

Because midnight in Whitehorn meant kisses all around. Men kissing Lori.

Josh kissing Lori.

He swallowed. "Maybe we should head home," he said to her.

Her eyes widened with surprise. Perhaps even hurt. "Oh. Sure."

He wanted to kick himself. She didn't understand his sudden urge to leave the celebration. She didn't realize he was saving her.

"You can't go now!" Melissa protested, fanning herself with one slender hand. A waiter came by and dropped an armful of noisemakers and party hats on their table. She plucked one out of the bunch. "Stay, Josh, and we'll let you wear the king's crown."

"Thanks, but—"

"I'll take it. Hey there, folks." Wily Rick Weber appeared out of nowhere to grab the cardboard-and-glitter party hat from Melissa and nod at all of them in greeting. "I'll take your...date home too, Josh, if she wants to stay."

Josh studied Rick with distaste as the other man plopped the purloined crown on his arrogant head. Damn it. The only thing royal about Rick was that he was one royal pain in the ass. Obviously he'd been hanging around, just waiting for his moment to horn in, and Josh had been so focused on Lori that he'd missed the other man's presence altogether.

"She goes home with who she came with, Weber," Josh said coolly.

With a shrug, Rick pulled out the empty chair beside Josh.

"And that seat's taken," he added.

Rick's eyebrows rose. "Not at the moment," he answered. Then he smiled at Lori, as if Josh wasn't there. "Happy New Year, Lori. You look incredible."

"Thank you."

She handled the flattery so calmly that Josh couldn't believe he'd thought he was being considerate by not complimenting her himself.

"Are you having a good time?" Rick asked her.

"Yes." Her smile was so pretty, so genuine, that he couldn't blame Rick for angling his chair even closer. She glanced at Josh, a teasing light in her eyes. "Josh is a first-rate escort, even if he doesn't dance."

Rick immediately straightened. "Dance? Did you want to da—"

"Dance?" Melissa broke in, putting the brakes on the request about to come out of Rick's mouth.

Josh wanted to kiss her.

Until she continued talking. "You must have misunderstood, Lori. Josh loves to dance. He's one of the few men I know who truly does."

Lori's smile died and her expression turned doubtful. "Oh, but—"

"He's getting old, though," Rick interjected

smoothly. "Now me, I must be a good four or five years younger than ol' Josh and I'd be happy to show you what youth can do on the dance floor."

"Ol' Josh" set his back teeth. Rick had graduated from high school a year ahead of him. "Weber," he started, a warning in his voice.

"You wouldn't want Lori to play the wallflower just because you're one, would you, pal?" Rick asked.

Backed into a corner, Josh wondered if it was possible to commit murder with a coffee spoon. What the hell was he supposed to do? Look like a caveman, like a caveman with possessive rights, and say he didn't want Lori to dance? She wouldn't thank him for that.

Rick stood up, smiling and holding out his hand to her. "They're playing our song," he said.

She stilled, her gaze darting toward Wyatt and Melissa. Josh could see those wheels turning in her head again. She was just beginning to make some friends in Whitehorn and she didn't want to offend or appear stuck-up by turning down what looked like a perfectly innocent offer. Slowly, she rose to her feet, the only sign of her discomfort in the deep-blue depths of her eyes.

Josh rose too, unsure what to do.

"*Oh!*"

Their heads all swung toward Melissa.

"What's the matter, honey?" Wyatt said.

"I...um..." A strange expression crossed Melissa's face. "I need...I need Lori in the powder room."

Lori blinked. "Are you all right?"

Melissa stood and grabbed Lori's arm, then pulled her away from the table. "I will be." She looked over at the astonished men. "It's a...it's a female problem," she said, then rushed the two of them off.

The three men left alone at the table didn't meet each other's eyes. "I think I'll, um, just be getting back to my own seat," Rick said, obviously suffering from the same inadequacy Josh was feeling at the mention of a problem exclusively "female."

As the other man departed, Josh settled back in his chair. Then he cleared his throat. "I hope everything's okay," he ventured.

Wyatt's mouth twitched. "I'm certain of it," he said. "In case you didn't notice, Melissa's womanly antennae were quivering from the moment Rick arrived."

"Huh?"

Wyatt chuckled. "I think the 'female problem' that suddenly came over Melissa was the need to get Lori off the hook of dancing with Rick."

Josh laughed. "Damn. Remind me never to malign female intuition again. And may I tell you I'm in love with your wife?"

Wyatt grinned. "Get in line, buddy. Get in line."

Josh grinned back, even as he realized that though Lori had been saved from dancing, they still had another bridge to cross. There was still midnight to come. There was still that kissing to avoid. He sighed.

By the time the two women came back, wearing identical, innocent expressions, the rest of the people at their table had returned. Everyone was wearing a hat and clutching a noisemaker. Lori and Melissa donned matching silver headbands that were fair renditions of the Statue of Liberty's headgear.

Handing them each a plastic horn, Josh was suddenly struck by their similarity. Both on the tall side, slender, with dark hair and blue eyes, there was something about the set of Melissa's features that was echoed on Lori's face. "You know, you two..." he started.

"Ten! Nine! Eight!" His comment was drowned out by the bandleader at the mike. The room took up the chant.

As Josh watched, Lori's face lit up and she joined in. He sidled closer to her, not touching, but close. When the smooching began, he'd hustle her toward the door. With any luck, she'd be so glad he wasn't getting her in a liplock that she wouldn't mind not saying goodbye to their group.

"Happy New Year!"

The resulting cacophony was deafening. Horns blared, toy drums were thumped, wind-up noisemakers squealed. Lori dropped her blower to hold her hand over her ears. She met Josh's gaze, her wide smile tipping up the corners of her eyes. Her mouth moved.

"What?" he yelled, leaning forward.

"I said," he could barely hear her, though she leaned toward him too. "Thank you. This is so much—'' the noise around them suddenly died. ''—fun.''

They both froze. Lori's eyes widened as she took in the kissing couples all around them.

A deer caught by headlights would appear less startled.

''Lori,'' Josh said softly.

Her gaze jumped to his.

''It's all right,'' he said. ''I won't. But another man might. So maybe we should—''

''Too late,'' she whispered, glancing over his shoulder. ''Here comes Rick.''

''Oh, Lori.''

She half smiled. ''Oh, Josh.''

He only knew of one way to save her—he was here to rescue her after all. Still, he stalled. ''Someone hurt you, didn't they?''

She hesitated, then nodded.

He closed his eyes for a moment, opened them. ''I'm sorry. So damn sorry. But the truth is, though I don't want to scare you, I definitely want to kiss you.''

Her gaze flicked back over Josh's shoulder, then back to his face. She licked her tempting, tantalizing lower lip. ''You don't have—''

''Shut up,'' he said, moving close enough to enjoy her soft, evocative scent. No more nice guy, not with Wily breathing down his neck. Not with Lori, beautiful, creamy-skinned Lori in front of him. Josh leaned over her, ignoring her flinch.

''I won't touch you,'' he said gently, shoving his

hands in his pockets to prove it. "Not anywhere but—" his mouth settled lightly against hers "—here."

Peach brandy. Lori tasted just like peach brandy.

A relative had sent his folks a bottle one Christmas. It had sat in the cupboard above the oven, dusty and forgotten, until Josh was seventeen. Then, one night, with typical teenage idiocy, he'd unearthed it when his parents were out of town and a couple of buddies were over.

The initial sip had seemed harmless enough. Sweet, like a long, hot summer captured, then its essence extracted and candied. But even that first swallow had lingered on the tongue, heated up the belly, dizzied the mind.

So Josh wasn't thinking clearly when he ran his tongue across Lori's full bottom lip. Her mouth softened and he tickled her bottom lip again, pushing on its puffy center to encourage her mouth to open. She sucked in a sharp breath and he followed it with his tongue.

More heat, more sweetness. The taste of Lori's mouth rushed into him, into his blood. His hands fisting in his pockets, he angled his head for a better fit. Her mouth opened wider and that signal of willingness instantly hardened him. He edged closer, the tips of his shoes bumping against the tips of hers.

He thought they should breathe, but he couldn't make himself lift away from the delicious taste of her mouth. His tongue slid against the slick warmth of hers, his heartbeat banging like drums in his ears.

But over that, he heard her moan.

He stilled. The sound was soft, an entreaty, and a great flood of satisfaction ran through him. For a moment he'd forgotten her fears. And maybe she had, too.

The idea gentled him. He softened his mouth, made his tongue retreat from the seductive sweetness of hers. He separated their lips in a last, slow caress. Then he kissed one corner of her mouth. Then he kissed the other.

Then, letting out a long sigh, he lifted his head and stepped back.

Her eyes were closed, her head still tilted toward his. Slowly, her lashes rose. They stared at each other.

Lori put the back of her hand to her lips. She held it there, and he didn't know if she was trying to erase the feel of his mouth or press it more firmly to hers.

His heartbeat was slowing, his sense was returning, he remembered the piercing pain of the hangover that peach brandy could bring. Nothing so sweet, so potent, came without a price.

"Are you okay?" he asked.

Her hand dropped. Her mouth was rosy, darkened by his kiss. "I'm..." She shrugged.

A chill ran down Josh's spine. Maybe he'd misinterpreted her response. Her willingness. Hell, hadn't he had trouble reading her from the very beginning?

He swallowed. "Damn it, did I get it wrong? I thought you enjoyed it."

"I did."

At those two words, he stepped forward.

She instantly, instinctively, stepped back.

Josh froze. Of course one enjoyable kiss hadn't healed her. He rocked back on his heels, giving her more space without actually retreating, then scrubbed one hand over his face. "I think we might have a little problem."

She gave a nod, and he gave her credit for facing up to it. "We shouldn't have kissed," she said.

"I wouldn't go that far." Josh tried grinning, but he wasn't sure how successful he was. "The real problem is, I'm going to want to kiss you again."

Her eyes widened and she swallowed. "Josh—"

"So what are we going to do about it, Lori?"

She put her hand to her hair, encountered her Statue-of-Liberty crown, pulled it off her head. Her eyelashes swept down as she gazed at the hat. A wavy piece of her dark hair fell across her cheek. "I don't know, Josh. I honestly don't know."

Chapter Five

New Year, schmoo year, Lori thought. Instead of making a list of resolutions, she was going to make a batch of cookies. Chocolate chip. Ooey, gooey, can't-think-of-anything-but-how-good-they-taste chocolate chip cookies.

It didn't matter that it was only nine o'clock in the morning, New Year's Day. A bowl of oatmeal or a bagel and cream cheese wasn't going to cut it. Not this morning. Not when she had to get her mind off Josh and the fact that they'd shared a kiss.

A heartstopping, nerve-hurdling kiss. A kiss she could have sworn would scare her. And it did. Oh, God, it did.

Over the pass-through in her small kitchen, Lori could see the TV in her living room. As she gathered the cookie ingredients, she caught glimpses of the floats of the Rose Bowl parade sailing by. The commentators spoke non-stop, their voices full of studied, if not quite sincere, enthusiasm.

Lori had expected to react to the New Year's Eve party the night before with that same kind of gaiety—the kind one had to work at.

But she would have forgiven herself for it, because merely accepting Josh's offer to attend the celebration had been a big step all by itself. She was so accustomed to hiding—first, the kind of marriage she'd had, and later, from her ex-husband—that she usually said an automatic no to invitations and regretted it afterwards.

But Josh had breached Lori's walls by mentioning Melissa. Lori's reason for coming to Whitehorn had been to establish a relationship with her half sister, but she was wary of going to the other woman with the truth straight away. She badly, badly didn't want to be rejected by Melissa. Not when she needed the strength of family connections so much.

Damn David. Lori fostered the fiery spurt of anger against her ex-husband. Thumbing on the hand mixer, she vigorously beat the butter, eggs, vanilla and sugars together, watching them blend with a fierceness the innocuous ingredients didn't deserve.

Her anger leaped higher. She hadn't deserved to be hit by David. She hadn't deserved to be made afraid.

But she wasn't going to let him ruin her life forever. To ruin her.

And as difficult as it was to think about, last night's

kiss was among the first pieces of evidence that she *wasn't* ruined.

The kiss had been gentle, sweet and hot all at the same time. It had made something deep inside her clench, then release. A lovely melting that had made her feel like a woman.

But there was no telling how long and how far that feeling would take her. And certainly Josh didn't know what that brief meeting of lips represented to her. As kind and gentle as he was, she couldn't imagine explaining to him how much that one simple kiss had meant.

Of course, she couldn't imagine facing him in the office tomorrow either.

The first dozen cookies were just coming out of the oven when the phone rang. Lori started, staring at the phone. David hadn't found her here, had he?

Knowing was better than not knowing, of course, so she set down the hot cookie sheet and made herself cross to the phone. With a deep breath, she lifted the receiver, praying it wasn't a man's voice on the other end of the line.

But it was. Her spine wilted against the wall. It was a man's voice, all right. It was Josh's.

"Hello? Lori? Are you there?"

"Yes, yes. I'm here." She tucked the receiver between her ear and her shoulder and moved back to the cookie sheet, hoping the smell of the warm cookies would ease the rapid beating of her heart.

"I thought we should talk," Josh said.

In her mind's eye, Lori saw his mouth, she felt

again the way it had pressed against hers, the way he had coaxed her into opening for him. A shiver trickled down her spine.

No. She slid one of the cookies off the sheet and juggled it between her two palms, desperate for the taste of chocolate and brown sugar, counting on its can't-think-of-anything-else quality to block out the memory.

"Lori? Honey?"

The casual endearment plunged straight for her heart, so she took a huge, cleansing bite of cookie. A melted chocolate chip seared the surface of her tongue. She let out a strangled moan.

"Lori. Damn it. Are you all right?"

"Fen," she mumbled around the hot bite. She managed to chew, then swallow. "Fine. I was eating a hot cookie. I burned my tongue."

The sudden, charged silence on his end of the line made her close her eyes. There was no doubt where his mind was going—exactly where her mind had been.

"That's what I called to talk about," he finally said.

Burning tongues? she thought, almost giddy. But that brought her mind back to their kiss. "It was a mistake," she said hastily.

Josh's voice was dry. "Burning your tongue?"

Lori closed her eyes, feeling stupid. Embarrassed. "That too," she answered.

"It was just a kiss, Lori," he said.

Another wave of embarrassment rolled over her,

followed by a second wave, this one of relief. Just a kiss. Of course, it was just a kiss in his mind! While she was seeing it as some kind of personal emotional barometer, to Josh it was just a kiss. Lips meeting lips. Yes, there'd been some tongues involved too— burning tongues—but on New Year's Eve, people kissed. Even with tongues.

He didn't see it as a pivotal moment, as an emotional statement.

For him it was "just a kiss."

Lori cleared her throat. "You're right," she said. "There's no reason to make a big deal about it."

"Good," Josh said heartily, though the heartiness sounded a bit forced, like the soap-star parade host on the nearby TV who was currently describing the latest float going by with its "dozens of beautiful, waving mermaids in spectacular scales made of shiny and fragrant citrus leaves."

Lori rubbed at the center of her forehead, telling herself she was imagining things. "I'm sorry, Josh. I hope I haven't made *you* uncomfortable."

"Nah. But I didn't like starting a new year with an awkwardness between us. You're sure you're okay?"

"Of course." She let herself relax. "Believe it or not, you don't have to treat me like something made of glass."

He laughed. "You're talking to the man whose windpipe you nearly broke a week ago. I know *exactly* how to treat you."

"And how is that?"

"With caution, honey. With caution."

This time the endearment wasn't so wrenching and she laughed. Knowing that Josh didn't find anything special in their kiss made everything so much easier for her. "Thanks, Josh."

"For what?"

"For the call. For taking me to the party last night. I haven't had a...normal time like that in a long while."

"Is that so? What makes something 'normal' for Lori Hanson?" he asked.

Lori picked up one of the cooled cookies and nibbled at the edge. How had things been, how had *she* been, before her mother's illness and before David came into her life?

"Friends," she said, then sighed. "I left a lot of them behind right after college. My mother had moved to the northern end of the state, and I went there to take care of her when she became ill."

"Ah," Josh said. "What else?"

"Laughter, I suppose." She swallowed. "Later... later I didn't find that much to laugh about."

"What did you like to do, when things were normal?"

"Oh, I don't know. What do people do who have just gotten out of college? Hang out? Go to the movies?" She remembered the last day of what had been her "normal" life. In the evening her mother had called her and told Lori about her cancer diagnosis. But that afternoon... "I loved to go for walks in the rain."

Josh was silent a moment. "Hmm. Well, no rain

in Whitehorn today. No snow coming down, either. But if you'd like to do something outdoors...."

"Oh, I—" Lori swallowed her immediate refusal, reminding herself that she was in Whitehorn to make changes. "What did you have in mind?"

"Would you like to go sledding?" His voice held a boyish note.

Lori found herself smiling. "Sledding? I don't know how to sled."

"No one knows 'how' to sled. You just sled. You sit down, point yourself south, and hold on."

"You don't steer?" she asked.

"You won't have to steer," Josh answered. "I'll do the steering for you."

Let Josh steer her? She'd let herself be controlled by many things in her life, by circumstances and then by her husband, and look what a disaster that had been. But this was Josh. Big, kind Josh, who she...trusted.

Her heart lurched in her chest. She *did* trust him.

And she could. It was really okay. Because he'd told her there was nothing special about their kiss. He didn't expect anything more from her.

Suddenly Lori felt like one of the giant balloons in the New Year's Day parade. Buoyant, as an unfamiliar eagerness, an excitment for life, filled her. "When do we go?"

Dozens of people congregated in and around the sledding area. Cars were parked below a ten-foot bank of plowed snow. Just a few feet from the edge of the bank sat spectators in lawn chairs, steam curling from their thermos cups of hot coffee and cocoa as they lifted their faces to watch those sliding down the hill directly ahead.

Dressed in her warmest clothes, Lori climbed up the steep slope behind Josh. He carried the sled under one arm and turned to check on her from time to time. Despite the alarming speed of the kids whizzing past them on various pieces of snow paraphernalia, Lori managed to smile brilliantly at him each time.

Surely they wouldn't move as fast. Besides, she trusted Josh.

Their first run was as exhilarating as she'd imagined. Josh sat behind her, and she didn't mind at all leaning back against the wide wall of his chest. The cold air slapped her cheeks as they slid down the hill—at a decorous, yet still exciting pace—and when they shushed to a stop, she couldn't wait for another turn.

It only made it better to realize no steering was involved at all. Other than making sure their sled wasn't pointed in the direction of a particularly treacherous-looking icy patch, Josh just pointed the thing downward and allowed them to slide away.

The next ride was even more fun.

At the top of the hill, preparing for their third run, Lori couldn't help but turn to look back at Josh, seated behind her on the sled. Her shoulder braced against his chest, she grinned at him, knowing her cheeks and nose must be as red as his. "This is great!"

He didn't smile back. He didn't nod at her either. What he did do caused her heart to leap into her throat, and it stayed there, hammering against her skin.

His gaze focused on her mouth. Sharpened.

Lori swallowed. "What?" she said.

His nostrils flared. "Your mouth. It's…flushed. It was like that last night."

Lori's body heated beneath her parka. "It was cold last night, too," she said.

"Not the cold." He shook his head. "It wasn't the cold that made your mouth that way. It was mine."

Lori remembered putting the back of her hand to her lips. She remembered feeling the heat that he'd left behind. "It was just a kiss," she whispered, her voice gone suddenly hoarse.

Josh opened his mouth, but then the sledders waiting behind them shouted for them to get moving. Lori faced forward, preparing for their run.

Josh's heels dug into the snow to propel them forward. Just as he pushed, Lori looked over her shoulder. "You said it wasn't anything special."

Her comment caught Josh by surprise, that was obvious. His whole body jerked, the movement starting them moving, faster than ever before. His movement also altered their path, heading them straight for that slick path of packed, icy snow he'd been so careful to avoid before.

Lori gulped, their speed several notches higher than previously. The dots of colored parkas around them began blurring. "Josh!" She was afraid to turn and look at him. She was afraid to look ahead. Their speed increased, and her eyes squeezed shut.

A shout forced them open. Instead of slowing at the bottom of the run as they had before, their increased momentum had them heading straight for the line of spectator-filled lawn chairs. People scattered, dragging their chairs with them, leaving Lori, Josh and their sled with a clear path to...

Air.

They hung in it, forever it seemed, as they flew off the edge of the ten-foot snowbank that dropped to the parking lot below. Then *they* dropped. Bounced.

The sled skittered off in one direction. Lori landed on her back in a cloudy pile of snow. Then, as if they were fated to this pose, Josh half-fell on top of her.

She gasped. He quickly shifted, rolling to pull her on top of him. His hands fell back to the snow.

Cold nose to cold nose, they stared at each other. His face was grim. "Damn right it was special," he said.

Then, without using his hands to hold her in any way, he lifted his mouth. And kissed her. His lips were cold, but his tongue was hot.

Lori shuddered. *He thought their kiss was special.* Too.

Oh, it was scary how good that sounded. He slanted his head, taking the kiss deeper. Lori's body softened against his.

Softened. She'd gone *soft*.

Wrenching herself away from his mouth and away

from Josh's powerful body, she jumped to her feet. "I think we should go," she said, her voice tight.

He dropped his head back into the snowdrift and closed his eyes. "Okay. Just give me a minute."

Lori swallowed, now concerned. "Are you all right?" The snow pile had cushioned her fall, but maybe Josh's landing had been more jarring.

One of his eyes opened. "Sooner or later I will be, I'm sure." Then he smiled at her, that big, sweet one that seemed to melt the snow beneath her feet.

Lori's insides went to mush again, too.

She spun in the direction of his car, the soles of her snowboots slipping in her haste to put distance between them. Kisses, special kisses, were one thing.

But going soft was another thing altogether. Going soft was way, way too costly.

Josh either didn't detect or ignored Lori's agitated reaction to their second kiss. On the way back toward town, she stared out the passenger window, pretending an interest in the snowbanks the plows had left on the side of the road.

Josh slowed the car at an intersection and glanced at her. "Do you mind if we stop by Melissa and Wyatt's?" he asked. "I told them I'd drop by today to pick something up."

She should refuse. She should want to get away from Josh and his dangerous ways as soon as possible. But he was offering her another chance to see Melissa, she reminded herself, even as she nodded.

Knowing how treacherous he was to her should keep her safe enough.

The Norths ushered them into their large, warm ranch house with sincere delight. Melissa sent the men off into the den with a bowl of popcorn and another of potato chips, while she urged Lori into a seat at the table in the cheery kitchen decorated in accents of blue and white.

Melissa smiled at Lori. "Thank goodness you're here."

Though puzzled, Lori couldn't help but smile back. "Why is that?"

"Our son Tim is staying with a friend for the weekend, leaving me alone with Wyatt, a man who has only one thing on his mind." She rolled her eyes. "Football. Do you have any idea how many games there are on TV today?"

Lori shook her head, amused. "I can't say that I do."

Melissa sighed, setting two cups of tea on the table. Then she fetched a plate of cookies and sat across from Lori. "You've never been married then," she said.

Lori looked down at her teacup. "As a matter of fact, I have."

"Oh." Melissa was silent for a long minute, then her hand came over Lori's free one. "I'm so sorry for your loss."

Lori's head jerked up. "Oh. He's not dead." She looked back down. "But our marriage, it's over."

Melissa's gaze didn't waver. "And it wasn't a happy one."

"No. We've been divorced for three years."

Melissa pushed the cookie plate Lori's way. "So you gave up on men?"

"Oh, I don't know..." Lori shrugged. "I don't think I've really given any man..."

"A chance?" Melissa supplied. "That must be a pretty tall order, rebuffing the ones who try. You're very beautiful, you know." A mischievous smile curled her lips. "Wyatt even mentioned it to me, and he knows I'm the jealous type."

The gentle teasing warmed Lori. This camaraderie, this sense of warm acceptance was why she'd sought out her sister. "I don't think you need to worry, though," Lori said. "It's very clear Wyatt has the woman he wants."

Melissa smiled, and lifted her teacup in a toast. "To men."

Lori shook her head, as she raised her own cup. "To your happy marriage." She sipped, then let out a little sigh. "It must feel great to have done it right, to have made the right decisions."

Melissa sat back in her chair. "Yes. Finally, we did."

Lori's eyebrows rose. "Finally?" Then embarrassed at what must sound like prying, she leaped into an apology. "I'm sorry, it's none of my business."

"It's all right." Melissa scooted her chair closer to the table. "It's not a secret, and in Whitehorn we couldn't keep it one anyway. While he's a year older than me, Wyatt and I were high-school sweethearts. We planned to get married after I graduated.''

''But something happened?''

A shadow passed over Melissa's face. ''My senior year my mother and I moved to California. The separation was difficult for me and Wyatt, though we still loved each other and we still wanted to be together desperately. But my mom needed me in California, Wyatt was in college in Montana, and the time apart kept stretching longer and longer. Then one night Wyatt went to a party with a college buddy. Too much to drink, a beautiful woman who seemed to ease his loneliness, and one night later that beautiful woman—the daughter of a state senator—was pregnant.''

Lori swallowed. ''Then Wyatt…he…''

''Married her,'' Melissa said. ''Six years later they were divorced, and Wyatt came back to Whitehorn, having no idea that I'd returned too, and opened the Hip Hop. It was quite a…reunion.'' Melissa grinned.

Lori found herself fascinated. ''What happened?''

''Well, for one thing, he kidnapped me.''

Lori jerked back, the idea of Wyatt forcing Melissa to do something against her will disturbing. ''No!''

Melissa chuckled. ''It sounds drastic, I know, but the truth is, he thought it was romantic.''

''It's never romantic to be coerced into something.''

The good humor in Melissa's eyes extinguished. ''Oh, Lori.'' She reached out and touched the back of her hand. ''It wasn't exactly like you're thinking.

The only thing Wyatt really forced me into doing was listen to him. And the truth is, we needed to talk about what had happened between us in order to get beyond our past mistakes, our past hurts.''

Lori nodded. ''Okay. I'm glad he didn't…didn't hurt you.''

''Never. Not once in the way you mean,'' Melissa said, her vehemence touching. ''We have a strong marriage. We have a son. We have a love that was tested, but that survived.''

Lori blinked at the tears stinging the corner of her eyes. ''So there really is a happily-ever-after?'' she said lightly, ignoring the lump in her throat.

''If you find the right man. If you understand that every moment won't be happy, but that you want to share all the happy moments you *do* have with him.''

Lori had to blink again. ''You should start a column. Advice for the lovelorn.''

Melissa grinned. ''Believe it or not, I don't usually spill my views on love and marriage like this. But with you…'' She shrugged.

That wonderful feeling of warmth and friendship glowed like a light inside Lori. ''Thank you,'' she said.

''You might not want to be so grateful quite yet,'' Melissa answered, wagging her finger. ''Because I'm feeling an undeniable urge to matchmake too, or at the very least, pry. What's going on with you and Josh?''

''He's my boss.''

''And what else?''

"Nothing," Lori said, banishing the memory of his mouth against hers, the mild scratch of his whiskers against the edge of her lips. "He's just being kind to me."

"Oh, yeah. That's exactly how I would describe the kiss you two shared last night. It was definitely a 'kind' kiss."

"He scares me," Lori blurted out.

Melissa froze. "Josh scares you? I know he's giant-sized, but he doesn't have a mean bone in his body."

His bones were long and strong and covered with warm flesh that smelled of a tantalizing, delicious spice. His kisses were delicious, too. Lori couldn't tell her half sister that Josh scared her because he was *too* delicious, *too* tantalizing. That he made her soft, and she couldn't afford to let down her guard that way again. "It's just that my ex-husband…" Her voice trailed off, and she lifted her hand, let it drop.

Melissa was silent a moment. "Wyatt hurt me too, Lori. But I learned that I couldn't let the past over-shadow my life. I couldn't let it jeopardize my future happiness."

Lori wondered what Melissa would say if she confided that the way her ex-husband had hurt her had broken more than her heart. She opened her mouth, but then closed it as Wyatt and Josh trooped into the kitchen.

"Are you ready to hit the road, Lori?" Josh asked.

Lori stared up at him. Stacked in his arms, all the way to his chin, was a lifetime's supply of rolls of gift wrap and spools of ribbon. As she watched, the topmost cylinder of red curling ribbon wobbled, and he used his chin to stabilize it.

"What's all that?" she asked.

His expression looked a little embarrassed. "It's wrapping paper. Ribbons and stuff."

One of the rolls appeared to be pink, and decorated with baby-blue sheep. "There's your scary man," Melissa murmured. "He bought one hundred and fifty dollars' worth of stuff from our son Tim. I don't think he even looked at the boxes he checked off on the order sheet."

She rose from her seat and approached Josh. Standing on tiptoes to kiss his cheek, she tucked a roll farther back in the stack. "The next time I need to wrap a present for St. Patrick's Day, I'll know who to call."

"Give me a break," Josh muttered. "It was a fundraiser. Tim was wearing his 4-H uniform."

Melissa smiled at him. "You are one dangerous man," she said, then shot a meaningful look at Lori. "One dangerous man."

The dangerous man drove Lori home, the gift wrap and ribbons rolling around in the back seat of his SUV. When he pulled up in front of her apartment building, he cast her a hopeful look. "You wouldn't happen to have some baby showers or bridal showers or St. Patrick's Day parties in the offing, would you?"

And despite everything that had happened between them, despite every resolution she'd made and every warning she'd given herself, Lori laughed.

She was still grinning as she let herself into her apartment. It was so hard not to, even though at the sound of her laughter Josh had gone suddenly serious instead of joining in.

Chapter Six

Damn, Josh told himself, driving away from Lori's apartment. This was no laughing matter.

The woman could knock the air out of him with a look, or even a chuckle, as easily as she did with her forearm against his windpipe. He'd thought he was smarter than that.

But his reaction to Lori wasn't coming from the vicinity of his brain. His brain knew that he didn't want the complications of a relationship with someone who worked for him. With someone who'd been hurt by another man. With someone who made him feel so protective, which in turn made him feel so damn...

Vulnerable.

He conjured up his late wife's face. Kay had

brought out similar feelings in him and look where that had led. Kay had laughed at his attempts to protect her, laughed at all his warnings and admonitions.

Then she'd broken his heart with a wedge of grief when she'd died taking a foolish risk.

But Kay wasn't Lori.

More important, Josh wasn't the same. He wasn't going to fall in love again.

So, didn't that make things safe between him and Lori? He thought she was beautiful and sexy, no doubt. He admired her strength, her courage in moving to a new place and making a life for herself after what must have been a difficult—Lord, the understatement!—experience. Why shouldn't he want to help her?

He was patient. And after growing up with three sisters, he had a more-than-healthy respect for women. He had always possessed a certain rapport with them as well. Put like that, it was almost his duty to play Good Samaritan and bring Lori out of her shell.

Neither one of them wanted to risk their hearts, he was sure of that. But for Lori to find passion in a man's arms—wasn't that something worthwhile to aim for? Okay, it might be a little arrogant that he thought he knew what was best for her, and more than a little arrogant to think she could find aforesaid passion in *his* arms, but he'd kissed her.

He knew what mutual arousal tasted like. He also knew when it was an arousal worth pursuing.

And as he'd noted before, he was a patient man.

* * *

The following week at work, Josh found himself calling upon that patience a dozen times a day. Lori's perfume would drift by the door of his office and he'd lift his head like a dog on the scent. She'd hand him some papers, and he'd be forced to stare at her long, slim fingers instead of giving away his attraction to her by meeting her eyes.

The sound of her smooth Southern accent could tie him in knots.

Her smile caused him to break pencil leads.

One morning he watched her lick stamps, and his biological response forced him to stay behind his desk and think of ice baths for the next half hour.

He'd never considered himself a man with a limited tether, but now he was worried he was nearing the very frazzled end of his.

The notion that he didn't know himself as well as he'd thought put him in an extremely bad mood. The men on his work crews sidestepped whenever he came near. His foremen recommended he remain in the office instead of visiting the job sites, when the whole reason he was visiting the damn job sites was so he could stay away from the office.

It was after one of these frustrating trips—this time Jim, his foreman on the Hip Hop project, had virtually ordered him out of his hair—that he returned to an empty receptionist's desk.

Lori was bound to be about somewhere, but he checked through his messages before seeking her out. He was expecting to hear from a particularly cantankerous inspector, but the man still hadn't returned his call. Josh's foul mood growing even fouler, he stalked toward the coffee room, thinking more caffeine would probably kill him—putting them all out of his misery.

On his way there, movement in the one-person-sized supply room caught his eye, and he strode in without thinking. "Lori—"

She gasped, then spun around, her back against the metal shelving. Her mouth opened on a scream, but then *"Josh,"* came out instead. A little strangled, but his name all the same.

"Sorry for startling you," he apologized. His mind on the pain-in-the-butt inspector, he lingered in the doorway, lifting his arms to grip the ledge of the door-jamb. "Did we hear from—"

He broke off as he noticed her retreating farther into the shelving. "Honey," he said. "You're going to have a spine full of staples if you don't move away from there."

Her body froze, though her gaze darted to his face. Her eyes were wide, almost panicked he would think, if he hadn't been working so damn hard on his patience. He hadn't tried to kiss her or touch her all week, thinking she'd climb another step on the comfort-level scale if he backed off following that scorching kiss in the snow.

"What's the matter?" he said gruffly. "Did something…someone frighten you?"

She inhaled a deep breath, then she inched away—a scant inch—from the shelving. "I'm sorry, Josh. But it's…it's you."

He blinked. "Me?"

She swallowed. "You." She lifted a hand and waved it up and down, indicating his body. "You're blocking the exit. It makes me a little nervous."

He instantly dropped his arms. "Hell, Lori. I'm sorry."

She hugged herself, rubbing her arms with her hands. Josh looked down at his body, realizing that even with his hands at his sides, his six feet five inches of two-hundred-plus pounds filled the doorway. Blocked it.

He stepped back into the hallway.

She immediately exited the supply room, putting a good two yards between them. "Now," she said, pasting on a half-baked smile. "What do you need?"

A brain transplant. An infusion of high-caliber patience. Maybe, God help him, the good grace to forget this whole idea of rehabilitating the beautiful woman in front of him.

Lori wasn't just nervous around men, wary of passion, cautious of relationships, though she was all those things.

She was genuinely afraid of a man of his size. Of him. Of Josh. How, *how the hell,* was he supposed to get around that?

Lori smiled at the bank teller who handled the business transactions and thanked her for her time. After she'd confessed to Josh that he'd scared the dickens out of her in the supply room, he'd gruffly asked her to run out and make the Friday deposits.

She knew she'd hurt his feelings. The poor man couldn't help being built like a mountain, but she'd seen the regret in his eyes. She knew he finally understood.

When it came to kissing, he'd caught on immediately. Not once had he tried to hold her, touch her with his hands. Instead, he'd used the power of his mouth to paralyze her. Which had worked pretty darn well all by itself.

Lori returned to her car, gulping in great breaths of the cold, clean Montana air before ducking inside. It was a big country. Big mountains, big sky, big beauty. But for a woman who had to rely on her own strength to feel safe, big men toppled her sense of security.

David himself wasn't so large. She hoped—prayed—that after two years of what she considered "training," she had the skills to stop him if he found her again. She thought she could run faster than him now. And if he came up behind her, she could use her self-defense skills—including every dirty trick she'd been taught—at least to give herself a moment or two to get away.

She counted on her strength and willingness to fight back to surprise the heck out of her ex-husband. She'd been so passive the two times he'd hurt her before she left him. The first time because she was so shocked that such a thing was happening to *her;* the second time because she was so fiercely focused on getting it over with so she could get out of the house. Forever.

But Josh—the sheer size of him—deflated a lot of her confidence. Yes, she'd managed to overturn him that day on the track, but this wasn't about the logical, sensible side of her brain. Her wariness of his bigness was about instinct. It was about the fear that had eaten a hole in her heart.

She sighed as she opened the office door, wishing she could start the day over. Now not only was *she* uncomfortable with Josh's size, but she'd made *him* uncomfortable with her discomfort.

"I'm back," she called out, stepping into the reception area. Her feet halted and she stared at her desk. Something wasn't right, something she couldn't quite put her finger on. "Josh?" she called out, her gaze darting toward his office.

Through the doorway, she saw he was on the phone. He caught her eye, sketched a wave, then glanced back down at the yellow tablet on his desktop.

Lori frowned, rubbing her forehead. Something wasn't quite right in Josh's office, either, but she had no idea exactly what.

Deciding she was imagining things, she headed toward her desk, skirting the office chair that sat opposite it. She paused again, glancing down at the cushion's familiar, cheerful red plaid upholstery. Familiar, yes. But exactly right? No.

Shaking her head, she walked around to the open side of her desk. The top drawer slid out with its usual squeak, and she set her purse inside. Then she pulled out her chair and sat down.

Her feet dangled four inches off the floor.

"Lori, I need you to make a few calls, please." The yellow tablet in his hand, Josh exited his office to drop into the chair across from her desk. His brow furrowed as he stared down at the scrawled figures on the top page of his tablet. "Hell, if I can't read my own writing sometimes," he muttered.

Lori looked down at his bent head. She stilled.

She was *looking down* at his bent head. Really. She was. She could see that the part in his hair was crooked where it dead-ended into a springy cowlick at the very top of his head.

The cowlick was boyish. Endearing. But she shouldn't be able to see it. Not when she was her height, and he was his. Even when they were both sitting down, he towered above her.

"Lori?"

She blinked. "What?"

Josh looked up. He had to, to meet her eyes. "I asked if you would call Don Sheffield over at the lumberyard. Ask him to go over with you the order I made last week and get an estimated time of arrival on each item."

"Okay." As she dragged her own pad across her desktop to make a note, the heels of her shoes dropped off the backs of her dangling feet. Lori finished writing, then glanced over. "Um, Josh…"

But he was already back in his office.

Determined to get to the bottom of what was going on, she slid off the seat of her chair, her shoes *clacking* against the hardwood floor as her feet slipped back inside them. Then she paced around her desk, past that office chair Josh had just vacated.

The very low office chair. She paused, peering at it, then looked about to compare this particular chair to its matches scattered about the reception area. The chair was missing something—parts of its legs were gone. On this chair, on this one alone, the large rolling casters that made the big chair easily moveable—and taller—had been removed.

She tried to think of what it had been like that morning. Casting her mind back, she tried remembering if the chair behind her desk had been different then, too. Had the cleaning crew who worked overnight somehow raised the height of her adjustable steno chair, while lowering this one? Why?

Shaking her head, she approached Josh's office. His head was down and he was still muttering over whatever he'd written on the tablet. When she lightly rapped on the doorjamb, he gestured her in without looking up.

"There's something fishy going on around here," she said.

He didn't look up right away, so she crossed her arms over her chest and came closer to stand between his desk and *his* visitor's chair. "Josh?"

"Just a sec," he said, scratching some figures on another sheet of paper.

Lori lowered herself to the chair across from his desk. When *her* seat encountered *its* seat sooner than expected, she swallowed a little hiccup of surprise.

Her feet were dangling off the floor again.

From her unfamiliar height, she had another endearing view of Josh's irregular part. Okay. For sure, this chair was higher too. The chair Josh was sitting in, again, was lower.

When he looked up, grinning at her, she thought she at least understood *who* had engineered the perplexing changes.

"Okay, Cheshire Cat," she said, though still puzzled about the why of it all. "Alice isn't quite clear on what this little adventure in Wonderland is all about."

He shrugged, his smile fading to an expression infinitely more serious. "I thought if I gave *you* a chance to be bigger, you wouldn't mind so much that under most circumstances, *I* am."

Lori felt her heart swoop, sliding down another unexpected rabbit hole. She made a mental grab for it, astonished that it would go off on its own like that, without the permission of her head, without its usual, instinctive watchfulness.

But, as if her heart knew that Josh—funny, sweet, sexy Josh—waited to cushion the fall at the other end, it continued on its path. Her toes on the brink of something deep and scary, Lori just managed to keep the rest of herself from tumbling heedlessly after it.

No, no, no. She wasn't going to fall.

That evening after work, however, she baked.

Staring at the cooling apple pie, it took but a second to think of the best way to get the tempting treat out of her apartment—and off her thighs. She'd take it to Josh.

Though she still searched the shadows of the lit walkway between her apartment and the adjacent carport, she found herself smiling at the idea of what she'd do if someone accosted her. A pie in the face, no?

She was still smiling as she used her elbow to knock on Josh's front door. He lived not far from her own apartment, in a small but charming house that had the air of an alpine lodge. Under the cheery light beside the door, the apple pie she held in both hands gave off the delicious smell of cinnamon as steamy tendrils curled into the night air.

No one answered the door. Lori used her elbow to knock again.

"Can I help you?"

The female voice had Lori whipping around. Another young woman came up the walkway behind her, carrying a platter of cookies. Her expression was surprised. "Are you here to see Josh?" the other woman asked.

Lori nodded dumbly. The unfamiliar woman facing her looked younger than Lori, diminutive and beautiful. She had medium-brown hair that swept her shoulders in a wealth of bouncy layers. In jeans, parka and suede boots, she looked perfectly dressed for Montana…and perfectly at home.

The at-home woman stepped past Lori and juggled her cookies so she could press the bell. "He probably has the stereo up too loud," she said.

Lori stepped back, unsure what to do. Then the door swung open, and a sock-footed Josh smiled at the sight of the cookie-bearer. "Julie!" In a smooth move that bespoke long practice, with one hand he swept away the cookies. With the other, he dragged the young woman toward him for a warm embrace.

He has a girlfriend, Lori thought. *Of course he has a girlfriend.* She stepped back again, farther into the shadows the outside light didn't reach. As soon as the other two went inside, she'd skedaddle back to her car.

The apple pie was looking tastier and tastier all the time.

As Lori took another step back, Josh held the young woman in his arms away. "I smell apple," he said, sniffing appreciatively and looking down at the plate she'd handed him.

Julie shook her head, her voice amused. "Those are chocolate. You've got an embarrassment of riches tonight, big guy."

Frowning, Josh looked at Julie, then past her, squinting into the darkness. "Hello?"

Her face burning, Lori was forced to come forward. "I, um, I'm sorry to interrupt." So what that she'd considered New Year's Eve and the day after a date of sorts? Josh hadn't touched her since, and the reason was obvious. His girlfriend had returned to town, or was back in the picture. Whatever.

Lori thrust the pie toward Josh's midsection. "This…this is for you. Not for any particular reason," she added hastily, casting an apologetic glance in the direction of the other woman. "But I made it and I don't want to eat it."

"Oh, boy, that happens to me all the time," Julie said, grinning. "Except usually I break down and gobble whatever it is before delivery."

Both hands full of baked goods, Josh looked from one woman to the other. "Well, come in, you two."

"I shouldn't," Lori said.

"You will." Before she could get away, Josh had handed off the pie and the cookies to the other woman and was pulling Lori inside.

With the door shut behind all three of them, he looked at Lori, at Julie, at the baked goods, with a smug grin. "An embarrassment of riches, all right."

Julie laughed.

Lori felt another burn of embarrassment. "I should go," she said again.

Josh shook his head in mock exasperation. "Runt, would you tell this woman that I'm planning on eating pie and cookies, not her?"

Runt? It didn't seem a pet name for a girlfriend.

Julie laughed again. "If I knew who 'this woman' was, I just might."

"I'm sorry," Josh answered. "Lori Hanson, this is my cousin, Julie Anderson. Better known as the Runt."

Julie made a face at him. "Nice to meet you," she said to Lori. "My first piece of advice in dealing with mammoth man here, is to refuse to answer to Josh's deplorable nicknames. I'm short, hence Runt. My brother is Wheaties—that's the color of his hair. My sister is Trout.'' She shook her head. ''Don't ask.''

Lori found herself smiling. ''That sounds like your second piece of good advice.''

Within minutes the three of them were in Josh's kitchen. Lori resisted all temptation—she planned on keeping to that for the entire evening—while Julie and Josh bickered good-naturedly over the best slice of pie and the biggest cookie.

A chocolate smear at the corner of her mouth, Julie reached for a paper napkin from a pile on Josh's kitchen counter. The room, decorated in white with black accents, looked like nothing a bachelor—even a bachelor builder—would choose for himself. Lori wondered if Josh's mother, or sisters, even Runt or Trout, had helped him pick the up-to-date appliances and stylish backsplash of tile.

''I just came to say goodbye,'' Julie said. ''Back to college tomorrow.''

''We'll miss you.'' He reached out to tug on the ends of her hair. ''You'll call me if you have trouble in the statistics class?''

''Don't you doubt it. I wouldn't have made it out of calculus alive if it hadn't been for you.'' She shot a look at Lori. ''This man is a whiz with numbers.''

If a man as big as Josh could be said to squirm, well, that's what he did. ''Nah, it's just that I know how your little runt-brain works.'' Then his gaze narrowed. ''You made sure your car is ready for the trip?''

Julie nodded. ''Dad checked it out, Wheaties

checked it out, even Trout's new boyfriend checked it out.''

Josh blinked. "Trout doesn't have a boyfriend," he stated. "She's too young."

"Seventeen," Julie said.

Josh frowned. "No one told me about this at Christmas."

"Exactly." Julie smiled. "We didn't want to ruin a nice family holiday. They left it to me to break the news tonight. But Wheaties told me to tell you he's shaken the boy up, he's shaken the boy down, he's read him the riot act. Even Dad thinks the kid's okay."

Josh sighed. "I guess if Uncle Rod think it's all right," he muttered.

"We girls grow up," Julie said lightly. Then she leaned across the table and kissed Josh's cheek. "As much as we know it pains you."

"What pains me is worrying about you—and now Trout."

Julie smiled at Lori. "We're double cousins, you see. Our mothers married brothers. Josh seems to think it gives him the corner on over-protectiveness."

Though Lori smiled back, the obvious closeness of the cousins tugged at her heart. This is what she had hoped to find for herself. Family. Roots. Someone who would look out for you, who you could turn to when the chips were down.

It didn't surprise her in the least to find that Josh was part of a family like that. That he offered love and advice—not to mention academic help—when necessary.

The younger woman jumped to her feet. "Gotta go," she said, leaning down to kiss Josh again. She smiled at Lori, who also rose to her feet. "Be kind to Prince Charming, here."

Bemused at the steel beneath the light tone, Lori watched Josh escort his cousin to the front door. She had reached it herself just as Josh closed it behind Julie.

"Oops," Lori said as he swung around. "You shut the door too soon. I'm on my way out, too."

Josh leaned his shoulders against the raised wood panels. "You just got here." A lazy smile lifted the corners of his mouth. "You haven't let me thank you for the pie."

Lori swallowed. "It was to thank *you*," she blurted out. Her cheeks heated, but she continued on. "I…I can't tell you how nice I thought it was, what you did today."

"Nice?"

Lori nodded. "Nice."

Josh winced. "You don't know how much that word can hurt a guy."

She wasn't buying his act for a minute. "I happen to think 'nice' was exactly what you were going for today, Josh. And I happen to be very, very grateful for it."

"Yeah?" Slowly, so slowly, he reached out his hand and touched her cheek with his thumb. Lori didn't flinch, he moved that carefully. She couldn't move at all.

He dragged his thumb down her skin, over her cheek, against the line of her chin. "What if I don't feel so nice tonight?" His knuckles stroked her bottom lip.

"You're always nice," Lori answered quickly. With each word, her mouth brushed his fingers, and his rougher skin seemed to catch at the smoother skin of her lips. Her pulse started clanging like a fire alarm.

Because there was smoke, she thought dizzily. It trailed around them, curling like a rope, drawing them inexorably closer. Without knowing how it happened, without Josh using his hands to pull her toward him, she was there, leaning her chest against his.

His hands still at his sides, he drew in a long careful breath. It caused his solid chest muscles to rise against her breasts. To rise against her nipples that had budded, hard and tingling.

"Lori," he said softly. "I'm going to kiss you. But this time, this time I don't think I can promise I won't touch you. So…" He closed his eyes, as if fighting off a wave of something, then opened them. "So hold my hands, honey. Take them, hold them."

She could only obey. Not him. But what her own pulse was clamoring for. She caught his hands with hers. Their fingers entwined.

Oh, it was good. The strength, the warmth of Josh's hands, made her apprehensive and excited all at once.

Her blood rushed through her body, nervousness and desire traveling from fingers to toes to mouth.

Mouth. His was full and hard-looking, but she knew it was gentle. She knew its taste.

She wanted to taste it again.

The last, anticipatory moment was sweet. It was healing. It was so good to lift her lips and ask for what she wanted.

"Kiss me, Josh," she said.

His fingers squeezed hers as he lowered his head.

He wasn't gentle.

It didn't matter.

Her mind spun away as he took her mouth, took the kiss she'd asked for. His breath was hot against her lips, his tongue was sure. She opened wide for him. She opened for Josh.

The kiss went on. It wasn't one kiss, it was a string of kisses, each one hotter, deeper, another rung on the ladder that was taking her higher, higher. Wet heat trailed across her cheek and he found her ear, nipped at it.

Shivers rolled hot and steady down her back. Lori heard herself moan.

She felt Josh's fingers clench against hers. He found her mouth again, plunged deep.

The shivers redoubled. Her pulse was everywhere, throbbing insistently, drowning out whiny cautions, whispering fears.

Then his mouth gentled, even as she felt his heartbeat knocking harder against her breastbone. Afraid to lose her place, afraid he would stop kissing her altogether, afraid she'd never know what this was like, with Josh, she lifted their entwined hands.

Inching her body away from his, she placed his palms upon her breasts.

Chapter Seven

Josh froze, his mouth against Lori's, her hands over his as they lightly cupped the warm roundness of her breasts. His body throbbed everywhere, his hormones pounded insistently in his brain, telling him to hurry, telling him not to hesitate because she had put his hands there herself. He should take what she was offering, he should touch, squeeze, bare her so he could see what he knew would be beautiful.

Instead, he lifted his head and met her gaze. "Lori?"

"Please, Josh," she said hoarsely. Her hands clutched at his. "Touch me."

"I will," he promised. "And honey, I want to. But Lori—"

She went on tiptoe, pushing her breasts into his

hands, pressing her mouth against his. "Don't make me wait, Josh."

That did it. He angled his head to deepen the kiss. He flattened his palms to rub their centers against the hardened nubs of her nipples. She gasped, a sweet, needy sound, and her hands left his to tangle in the hair at the back of his neck.

He rotated his palms again, absorbing her heat and the fine trembling of her body. His lips left hers and trailed down her neck, using as his guide the tantalizing fragrance of hot peaches. He licked across her collarbone, his head pushing aside the open collar of her plain shirt.

His fingers went to its buttons and he didn't let himself think about what he was doing. There was no past, no future to worry about, nothing but her warm, peach-flavored skin and the excited cadence of Lori's breathing.

He unfastened the buttons one by one, moving slowly but steadily until he encountered the waistband of her jeans. Leaving the shirt tucked in, he slid his hands inside the open edges to run his bare palms around her slender ribcage. Her breath caught—that sweet and needy sound again—and he brought her against him once more, his hands pressing against the small of her back.

Her goose bumps rose beneath his palm. He closed his eyes to savor the sensation, and to savor the knowledge that he aroused her as much as she aroused him. He kissed the top of her head, then her temple, her cheek. When she lifted her mouth to his once more, he feathered his fingers across her back, then her ribcage to meet at the front clasp of her bra.

He considered stopping again. He considered waiting for her to ask him, or asking for permission himself, but that would be letting the past into their world again. It wasn't going to come between them now, damn it. Not when her cheeks were flushed and her mouth rosy from his.

In one quick move, he released the clasp and pushed aside the bra's cups, revealing...

Lust slammed like a fist into his gut.

He was a visual man. A man who saw things in his head and then built them with his hands. But he could never have imagined such perfection.

Never dreamed of touching something so luscious.

Lori's breasts were firm, full and tipped the same rosy-pink as her mouth. Her nipples were furled tightly, closed like a flowerbud against a frost, and he couldn't help but bend his head and take one into his mouth.

She arched into him as he mouthed it lightly, letting her get used to the sensation of his tongue against her. Her hands speared into his hair, tugging lightly, and Josh's restraint broke.

He sucked.

Lori moaned, her fingers biting into his scalp as she drew him even closer to the silky, peachy softness of her breast. His mouth still on her, he cupped the other breast in one hand, weighing it, then brushing his thumb against its nipple with quick strokes.

His blood thudding like a runner's footsteps in his

veins, he switched places with her, setting her back against the front door. With hands that were shaking, he pushed her shirt and bra straps off her shoulders. Still caught at her waist, the shirt fell toward her knees, while the piece of white lace that was her bra fluttered to the floor.

He stared at Lori, desire-stunned all over again by the beautiful visual image she made. Her head was against the door, her hair a dark cloud around her flushed face. Her eyes were a drowsy, desire-filled blue, her mouth parted for her fast breaths, her pulse visibly beating in her throat. Below that, her creamy skin rose into those glorious breasts, one still wet from his mouth.

The other begged for his attention.

Leaning down to give it, Josh placed his palms flat against the door, caging her. Lori stiffened.

But not in anticipation of his touch. That was instantly clear.

He quickly drew back his hands, stepping away at the same time. But too late.

Too late, because her arms were crossed over her naked chest. Too late, because her body seemed to be trying to burrow backward into the solid-core oak door. Too late, because there was fear—and tears—in her eyes.

Cursing himself, he took another step in retreat. His feet tangled in something, and he stumbled. Looking down, he cursed all over again. Somehow he'd managed to get his size fifteens caught in her bra. It was wound around his ankles like shackles.

His face burned. *Smooth move, Anderson.* Closing his eyes, he groaned. "Now would be a good time for a hole to open," he murmured, "and swallow me right up."

Miracle of miracles, Lori laughed.

Still, he didn't look at her. "Easy for you, honey. But this isn't a situation they cover in *Gentleman's Quarterly* or even in *Construction Digest.*"

She laughed again. The next thing he knew, she was kneeling at his feet, untangling him from the white satin and lace that had been her undergarment. Then she stood, her shirt once more buttoned to the neck. She crumpled the bra and shoved it in her front jean pocket.

"Josh, I—"

"Lori, I—"

They broke off. He wondered if they both didn't really know what to say, because neither of them started talking again. She bit down on her lower lip.

"Don't," he said abruptly.

Her gaze jumped to his. "What?"

He made a frustrated gesture. "Don't think whatever it is you're thinking. I know this is awkward, but…"

She hesitated. "You did look really cute all ensnared," she finally said. A little smile began to play over her lips.

Josh narrowed his gaze, his own mood lightening at her teasing tone. "*Cute* is a lot like *nice,* Lori. Can't you think of another word? *Rugged,* say? Or *manly?*"

Her laugh bubbled out, and he relaxed a degree or two more. "So," he continued. "Why don't we just forget the whole thing?"

Of course, he wouldn't. He'd work hard to banish the thought of himself tripping over her bra, but he'd never forget the sight of her nakedness, the taste of her in his mouth.

"That's the whole problem, Josh," she answered, her expression serious. "I'm having trouble forgetting."

"I know," he said. "But there's no hurry—"

"I need to tell you," Lori said, shaking her head. "We need to talk now."

Josh made coffee. Lori knew she wouldn't drink any, she was too wired for caffeine, but she welcomed the few minutes alone in his living room so she could gather herself together.

His touch had excited her. His kisses had beguiled her. His mouth on her breasts had nearly brought her to her knees.

And then the past had risen up, like a serpent swimming through the sea of her desire, and she couldn't avoid the piercing bite of memories. Memories of another man. Of being at another man's mercy.

Josh came in, carrying a tray, and placed it on the coffee table in front of the long leather couch she sat on. He handed her a steaming mug and took another between his own hands. As he settled in the opposite corner, he nodded at the tray. "Cream and sugar, if you'd like it."

To stall a bit longer, she doctored her coffee, then leaned back against the couch. Taking a deep breath, she forced herself to meet Josh's gaze squarely.

He looked…uncertain. She smiled a little at that, that big, masculine Josh looked worried. She took another breath, let it out slowly. "Tell me about your marriage, Josh."

He jerked against the cushions, his coffee sloshing dangerously close to the brim. "I thought this was about you."

His uncertainty and worry had changed to wary. To closed-off and private. Lori thought about heeding the signs he was putting up. It certainly would be a heck of a lot easier if she went away right now and they never spoke of this again.

Except there would be another day at work. There would be another moment when all she could think about was the heated, heavenly taste of Josh's mouth. Her attraction for him wouldn't die, and neither would her fears, unless she brought some things into the open. But she needed to know about *his* marriage if she could talk about hers.

"This *is* about me," she said quietly. "Please talk to me. I—I need to hear it."

Josh looked down at his coffee, staring into the depths of its blackness. "I was five years older than Kay. We met soon after she graduated from college and came back to the Whitehorn area. As to how we met—I rescued her when her kayak overturned one summer day."

He looked up, but not at Lori. His gaze was fixed

on the white wall facing them as if seeing a film of the past. "It was the precursor of everything to come, really. When I was able to right the kayak for her, she came up laughing. As wet as a drowned rat, but laughing." He shook his head. "She never saw how close she came to disaster that day, or any other time, really."

Lori swallowed. "And after that?"

"We started dating," he said. "She was so full of vitality. Always moving, always laughing, always teasing me about my stick-in-the-mud ways."

Lori tried telling herself it wasn't her right to bristle. But nothing about Josh was stick-in-the-mud. He was strength and goodness and had been able to arouse Lori's desires despite herself.

She stared down into her own coffee. "But...you were happy with her?"

"I loved her. I married her."

But had he been happy? Lori noted he hadn't said, and her heart ached with...what?

"We'd just passed our second wedding anniversary," Josh continued, "when she died."

"What happened?"

"It was an accident. Kay had plans to go rock climbing one Saturday. I was up to my eyebrows in a project in the next town and was working that weekend. She and a friend were going to partner each other, but that morning her friend called and cancelled."

He ran a slow hand through his hair, as if the telling of the story exhausted him. "I had already left for the job site, so I had no idea that Kay then decided to make the climb solo. I would have stopped her if I'd known, or gone with her—something. About halfway into the climb, she fell.''

Lori's fingers squeezed her mug. "And?"

"She died instantly.'' He closed his eyes. "It's been…hard getting over the loss.''

"I'm sorry, Josh.''

Some quiet moments passed, because Lori didn't know what else to say. Other than the truth. "What I've been working on is—is getting over my *marriage,*'' she finally said.

His gaze found her and she wanted to duck from its steady regard. Instead though, she forced the bald, ugly words out of her mouth. "He beat me.''

Josh's body twitched, though Lori knew he'd guessed the truth long ago. "Beat you,'' he echoed, his voice flat.

"I used to try to pretty it up,'' she said. "I'd say or think to myself, 'he lost control,' or 'his anger took over.' I'm not very proud of that.''

Pain crossed Josh's face. "God, Lori.'' He ran his hand down his face. "I don't know how to talk about this, what the right words are.''

Lori nodded. "Of course you don't. I don't expect you to have the right words.''

"But damn,'' Josh said, his voice low but vehement. "It makes me want to beg your forgiveness. I want to apologize on behalf of the entire male half of the population.''

Lori nearly smiled. Josh, wanting to take upon his

shoulders all the wrongs of the world. Now why wasn't she surprised? "It's not your fault though, Josh. Not any more than it was mine. Sometimes I slip and find I'm blaming myself, but I've known from the first, from the very first blow, that it was David, not me, who was in the wrong."

Josh sucked in a deep breath. "Tell me about him. As much as I'd like to pretend the bastard doesn't exist, I think I need to know."

Lori nodded. "But the story starts before I met David...are you sure you won't be bored by the life and times of Lori Hanson?"

Josh set his coffee mug on the tray and then slid closer to her. He took her mug and set it down, too. Then, still leaving a half-cushion between them, he reached forward and folded one of her hands into his. The warmth of his touch traveled toward her heart. "I think you know Lori Hanson fascinates me," he said. "Her life, her times, her smiles, her tears and everything in between."

Oh. He was so sweet. He'd hate that word, just as he hated being called *nice* and *cute,* but what he didn't understand was that it was those exact qualities that gave her the courage to get close to him. The desire to get over her fears. They were qualities that described a heart, a heart that was decent and good. Boy Scout stuff, maybe. But Lori had never considered Boy Scouts sexy, and Josh was that, too.

"Lori?" Josh ran his thumb across her knuckles. "You okay?"

"Yes," she said. "Or at least I hope I will be."

"So." Josh gently smiled at her. "Tell me about the day you were born."

She shook her head. "We don't have to go *quite* that far back. Though I was born and grew up in Dicken, South Carolina, and that *is* important."

"Okay. Beautiful Southern girl grows up in Dicken, South Carolina. Then…?"

"Then girl goes to college, studies business, listens to loud music, hangs out with her friends. Not necessarily in that order, by the way."

Josh's lips twitched. "Typical college kid. Now what?"

"My senior year, my mother sold our little house in Dicken and moved to a new town and a new condominium complex in the northern part of the state." Lori looked down. "Shortly after I graduated, we found out she had cancer and only a little time to live."

Josh squeezed her hand. "Goodbye carefree college days."

She nodded. "Yes. I left everything behind, my hometown, my college friends and moved in with my mother. I took care of her and we had a few last months together." That's when Lori had found out about Whitehorn and Melissa. Though the stories hadn't meant much to her at the time, as focused as she was on her mother's illness and her own imminent loss.

Lori looked down at her hand, engulfed in Josh's bigger one. "David Post had the condo next door to my mother's. He was charming, sympathetic. He did little things that wooed us both, like hunting down a video of an old movie my mother mentioned, then delivering it with flowers and dinner from our favorite take-out place. That's one of the hardest parts…."

"What is?"

She met Josh's gaze. "Not knowing if that was the real David or not. Was that part an act? Did he truly care for my mother? Did he really ever fall in love with me?"

"What do you think?"

Lori shrugged. "I'm still not sure. It felt real at the time, but I was vulnerable. We didn't know anyone in town but the oncologist and David. I didn't spend time with anyone but my mother, who was dying, and David. We married the last month of my mother's life, standing in her bedroom right at the foot of her bed. The only thing I now feel certain about is that at that moment my mother was happy. Sometimes just that makes the rest of it all right."

Josh's expression looked grim, but his voice was even. "What was the 'rest' of it?"

Lori took in a long breath. "Those first few months are hazy. My mother died and I was occupied with settling her affairs, selling her condo, going through her things. David seemed as charming as ever. He's an accountant and his job had stressful times, but then…"

"But then?" Josh prompted.

"I don't know what happened." Lori shook her head. "I have no idea if something triggered his suddenly explosive temper, or if he'd been covering it up all the other months. But it was a short, fast slide from shouting to throwing things to finally—'' She broke off, mad at herself for stopping, but unable to say it. "You know."

"He hi—."

"No!'' All at once, she hated the words coming out of Josh's mouth. All at once, she hated Josh painting a mental picture of what David had done to her. She jerked her fingers from Josh's grasp and covered her face with her hands. "I've changed my mind. I don't want you knowing about this."

"But I already know, Lori," he said. "And I don't think any less of you. On the contrary, I—"

"It only happened twice before I left him." If she kept her eyes squeezed shut, then maybe she could get through some of this. A rusty laugh came out of her throat. "'Only' twice. I can't believe I just said that."

Josh didn't say a word, but even with her eyes shut, Lori could feel him beside her. Emotions vibrated off him—outrage, sympathy, she didn't know them all.

"The first time," Lori said, forcing herself to continue, "I was so shocked that I just stood there. He slapped me across the face, then punched me. My lip split and one eye turned black. The sight of my blood seemed to sap his anger. He cried. He begged my forgiveness. He brought me ice, he went out and came home with flowers and a filet mignon to put on my eye."

Lori's stomach clenched, remembering. "What was I supposed to do? This was the same man who had stood by my mother's deathbed and married me. The same man who had stood beside her grave when we buried her. Of course I'd read about battering, about domestic violence, but that wasn't what was happening to *me*.''

Josh's voice was tight. ''And then?''

''And then.'' Lori paused. ''And then came the second incident, about a month later. I just stood there then too, taking it again. But this time, this time while he was hitting me I was thinking, planning, waiting for his anger to leave…so that I could.'' She opened her eyes. ''He went out for flowers and filet mignon again, and I went to the police.''

Josh was so quiet, that she finally had to look at him.

He was still, his body, his face, frozen. Only his eyes seemed alive and their gaze was trained on her face. ''Lori, I—'' he started, then broke off.

There was more to her story, but Lori didn't think she could continue without knowing what Josh was thinking. He'd said she fascinated him. She knew he was a decent, good man. But maybe she disgusted him now, with her dirty secret out, polluting the clean air of Montana. ''Tell me what you're thinking, Josh,'' she said. ''I can take the truth.''

''What I can't take…'' he said hoarsely, ''What I *need* is to touch you, Lori. I can't take hearing that without taking you in my arms.''

Oh. Lori felt the sting of tears in her eyes, she felt the tug at her heart. She thought she might die of the bittersweet ache of it when he held open his arms.

"I won't close them around you, honey," Josh said. "But if you would just get close to me I might be able to breathe again."

She surprised herself. Instead of hesitating, instead of having to *make* herself edge toward Josh, she found that she wanted to be near him too. Not in a sexual way—Josh had already proved that he could lure her with kisses—but she wanted to be near him for comfort.

To receive comfort.

No, she thought, amazed. As she laid her cheek against his chest and felt his heart beating against her ear, she realized she didn't need comfort. She wanted to give it. Not that Josh thought he needed it, she'd put money on that, but it felt so good—so decent, so nice, so sweet, so *normal*—to want to give a man something for the first time in a long, long while.

True to his word, Josh didn't put his arms around her. But she embraced him. She slid her arms around him and held on to this big, strong builder who had come into her life and knocked down so many of her walls.

One of his hands lightly stroked her hair. "Where do we go from here?" he asked.

Lori swallowed. He wanted to go somewhere from here? The thought infused her blood like caffeine, like a shot of liquor. Her reaction was so quick, so hot and dizzying, that she realized she'd been testing him.

The truth of it shamed her. "I don't know," she said, looking up at him. "I didn't think that far ahead. I didn't think you would...I thought..."

One of his eyebrows lifted. "You thought I would turn tail and run now that I know the full story?"

A pang of guilt pierced Lori. He *didn't* know the full story. "Josh—"

"I'm beginning to think you have a very low opinion of me," he said lightly.

She shook her head. "You know I don't."

"'Nice?' 'Cute?' And now 'coward?'" There was just the barest hint of humor in his eyes. His hand stroked her hair again, and the humor died, replaced by something far more serious. "Lori, I don't know what's happening here. But I do know I'm not running away from you. I hope you don't want to run away from me."

"I don't know what to say." She didn't.

"Say that you won't try to shut this—us—down. That you'll be open to what may happen between us."

"But I don't know how long—"

"I'm patient." He grinned. "And I'm devious. I know how you like to be kissed now. I also know how fast we both go up in flames. Don't think I won't find ways to remind you of that."

Lori's pulse started pounding, dizzying her brain. She sat away from him. "I can't guarantee anything, Josh."

"I'm not asking for guarantees." He rose off the sofa and held out one of his hands. "Except that you'll be at work on Monday morning."

Swallowing, she found herself putting her palm

against his. He drew her to her feet. "We'll work things out, honey, however that may be," he said.

The words sounded reasonable. Do-able. But as Josh walked her out to her car, Lori still peered anxiously into the darkness.

He opened her car door for her. As she slid in, he smiled, so big and confident. So strong. So darn gorgeous. "We'll take it slow," he said, then shut the door.

Lori locked it. Slow, Josh said. A chill slid down her spine. She only hoped they had that kind of time.

Chapter Eight

By the time Lori was driving to work on Monday morning, she'd half-convinced herself that the erotic interlude at Josh's house was just a dream. She didn't know what to think about the information they had exchanged Friday night or his idea that they should be open to what was happening between them.

He hadn't called, though.

After her workout in the gym on Sunday morning, she'd found herself leaping to the ringing phone in eagerness, only to sigh in surprising disappointment to find Melissa on the other end of the line. Melissa was putting together an impromptu wedding shower Tuesday night for Darcy Montague, one of the women who'd shared their table on New Year's Eve. Would Lori like to attend?

Glad to have something to think about besides Josh, she'd accepted, only to find herself mooning about him later that afternoon as she searched the small stores in Whitehorn for an appropriate gift for a bride. In a small boutique she'd stumbled upon a treasure trove of lacy nightwear.

Instead of focusing on what would suit Darcy's taste, Lori found herself examining each frilly piece and wondering what Josh would think.

Of Lori wearing it.

Holding a diaphanous, white baby-doll set in one hand and a sophisticated black lace teddy in the other, Lori imagined Josh's face as she modeled one, then the next. Her face heated at the mental picture, but excitement rushed through her all the same. Sexual excitement, yes, but also the thrill of feeling alive, young, feminine.

After years of looking over her shoulder, after years of sweating out her fears in the gym, training for an encounter with a man, it was good—okay, it was wonderful!—to dream about an entirely different sort of encounter altogether.

She hadn't denied herself the fantasy, but as she let herself into the office Monday, her stomach knotted. Maybe Josh regretted knowing what he did about her. Maybe Josh had reconsidered wanting to nurture the sparks that flew between them.

But when she reached her desk, she decided he hadn't. Though he'd penned a businesslike note stating he'd be out of the office until the afternoon, he made it quite clear he was thinking about her.

Josh had left her kisses.

Chocolate kisses.

One held down each corner of the note.

There were three at the bottom of her mug, sitting so innocently on the small counter in the coffee room.

Another sat precisely over the letter "L" on her computer keyboard.

While she opened Saturday's mail, she pondered why he'd chosen that particular letter. For Lori? For lust?

For lo— No!

The candies kept turning up in the most unlikely places. They lined up like soldiers on the top shelf of the supply cabinet. Others lolled in the half-dozen egg holders in the mini-refrigerator. At lunchtime, when she grabbed the spare set of gloves she left in her desk before going out to her car, more chocolates spilled out of them.

Staring down at the kisses, glittering like silver treasure across the surface of her desk, Lori couldn't help smiling.

The front door squeaked open. "Just what I hoped to see."

Josh. Her heart jolted, but Lori swallowed back her nervous eagerness. "What?" she said, calmly looking up. "Woman smiling over chocolate?"

He shook his head, his shaggy dark hair brushing against the collar of his parka. "Woman smiling is enough for me.'' The door clattered shut behind him, and he approached her, bringing with him the smell of cold air, sawdust and a maleness that was Josh's alone, a scent that she remembered from being so much closer to him.

He halted on the other side of her desk, studying her. There were questions in his dark-lashed, dark eyes. Questions and concern. ''You good?''

''Good?'' Lori tasted the word, tried it out in her head. Good implied…so many things. Good implied…exactly how she felt. She smiled again, this time at Josh. ''Yes. I'm very good.''

He nodded, as if more than satisfied with her answer.

''Thank you,'' she said, her hand indicating the candy strewn across her desk, ''for all this.''

He gave her a sheepish grin. ''Don't thank me. I bought them yesterday, a fundraiser for the Whitehorn High School marching band.''

Lori laughed. He charmed her so easily. ''Don't tell me, the drum majorette stopped by in full uniform.''

Josh shook his head, smiling. ''A lowly trumpeter. Male.''

''Ah.''

''I went to high school with his mother, though.'' Josh's eyebrows wagged. ''Now *she* could make batons flame, let me tell you.''

Lori laughed again. ''I think I'm jealous.''

Josh's face turned serious, going from charmingly

boyish to rugged, lethal manliness. "You have no reason to be. I thought about you all weekend, Lori. About how you make me burn."

Lori's pulse jumped and her face heated. Unsure what to say, she looked back down at her desk and started scooping the strewn candy into a pile of silver.

"But don't worry," he said. His hand reached out, stole a kiss. "I told you I was patient." Whistling a soft melody, he moved off to his office.

Lori listened to the carefree sound. She picked up a candy, unwrapped it, let the chocolate melt on her tongue. But her pulse didn't slow. She could still smell Josh. She could smell the delicious scent of him mixed with the decadent fragrance of chocolate mixed with an unmistakable smell, like sulfur, that was sensual sparks ready to explode into fire.

So he was patient. Great, Lori thought, her pulse still throbbing, the thick taste of chocolate only partly satisfying. What if she found out she wasn't?

The next day wasn't any better than the one before. Josh moved confidently about, never seeming the least affected by her presence. Lori, on the other hand, made up excuses to go into his office. She brought him coffee, making sure her fingertips brushed his on the exchange. She even found herself watching him drink it, her gaze focused on his mouth touching the heated ceramic rim of the mug.

When she dropped her pencil on purpose, just to

watch him bend over in those worn jeans of his to grab it for her, she declared herself shameless.

Now if she only had the guts to tell him.

She attended Darcy Montague's wedding shower Tuesday night after work, relieved to have something else to think about. The restaurant at the Whitehorn Country Club, usually open only on weekends in the winter, was staying open Tuesdays through Saturdays until the Hip Hop resumed its business.

The party was taking place in the club's small banquet room, and, as Lori walked toward it, she noted the almost-full regular dining room and that the small bar was doing quite a business as well. But it was the female laughter drifting out of the banquet room's half-opened French doors that drew her.

She paused in the doorway for a moment, smiling. It was the sound of another time, just as the heated sensations that Josh brought out in her were feelings of another time. A carefree time when the present was full of possibilities, when the future appeared as a rainbow in the distance, with joyous pots of gold at every ending.

Suddenly Melissa was there, linking her arm with Lori's and dragging her forward. "Don't just stand there, join in!"

Despite the other woman's friendliness, Lori hesitated. "I'm so new in town, I feel a bit like I'm intruding."

"Nonsense." Melissa continued tugging her toward the group of twenty or so chattering women. "We're always eager to welcome someone new."

Just as had happened on New Year's Eve, they did. Lori placed her gift on top of the pile in the middle of a table, then found herself instantly polled by a woman she'd never met before. Was it worse to be dumped on prom night or graduation night?

After adding her vote for prom night, Lori wandered to another group. A woman passed Lori a photo of a wrinkly infant wearing a why-did-you-make-me-eat-lemons? expression. In a hospital-issue cap and a teeny sleeper that read Property of Doting Parents, he? she? was adorable. Lori sighed in appreciation, then someone made a place for her at the table where the doting mommy was giving play-by-play details of the birthing process.

Glasses of wine were passed around and the childless women in the baby group groaned, gasped and gulped their wine at appropriate intervals. Then a new sound had the doting mommy turn. In another moment her arms were full of the infant whose journey into the world had just been described in excruciating detail. The sound of hearts melting into soup rushed around the table.

Food came next, then presents before dessert. As Darcy opened each one, Lori saw that she wasn't the only guest who'd chosen to give lingerie. Piece after beautiful piece of prettiness was held up, admired. Darcy's cheeks were pink and the group's laughter turned more teasing.

Someone passed around paper napkins and the partygoers rated the honeymoon outfits—holding up their scores like Olympic judges—on a scale of one to ten, one being "Not tonight, honey," and ten, "better than naked."

The best of them at math after a glass of wine, Lori appointed herself head judge. As slices of cake were being passed around, she clinked her plate with her fork for attention. With great solemnity, she cleared her throat and declared that Darcy's lingerie, on average, rated a 9.25.

The room shouted with laughter.

Lori sat down, triumphantly grinning. As the chattering resurged around her, she couldn't think of the last time she'd felt this at ease. Surrounded by women, surrounded by their warmth and laughter, Lori had found a place. Perhaps a home.

Melissa plopped down beside her and, as if it was the most natural thing in the world, grabbed a spare fork to filch a fat swirl of mocha frosting off Lori's piece of cake. "You don't mind?" Melissa said.

Remembering how Melissa had shared Lori's french fries too, her heart skipped like a little girl trying to keep up with her big sister. Lori shook her head.

"Thanks," Melissa replied. "I'm so glad you came."

"Me, too," Lori said. So glad she'd come to Whitehorn.

Along with Darcy and Melissa, she was among the

last to leave the party. Lori helped clean up, then, arms loaded with a stack of gifts, she followed Darcy out of the French doors, intending to take them to the bride-to-be's car.

The restaurant's dining room was quiet now, but Lori glimpsed quite a few people still in the bar. Smiling in the afterglow of the pleasant evening and concentrating on balancing her stack, she didn't notice when someone strode toward her.

"Let me help with that."

Big hands slid beneath hers. The gifts were transferred from her grasp to another's, where they rested, looking so much smaller now, against a large, wide chest. Josh smiled at her. "Did you have fun?"

Lori's mouth dried. Her guard was completely down, left behind somewhere between the new mother cradling her infant and Melissa sharing Lori's piece of cake.

Standing in front of her was Josh. Big, sexy, Josh, whose kisses tasted better than chocolate. Josh, who had inspired her to buy two decadent items of lingerie on Sunday afternoon—one for Darcy and one for herself.

She swallowed.

"Lori?" he asked, his brows coming together over his chocolate-brown eyes.

"Fun," she managed to get out, nodding. "A lot of fun." Her gaze jumped to his mouth, and couldn't seem to move away from it.

"Lori?" His voice turned tense. Tight.

Her name ran like a shiver over her skin. It suddenly felt tight too.

She risked a look into his eyes. "Josh...I..." All sorts of shameless ideas rolled through her mind. Chocolate kisses. Open-mouthed kisses. Where she wanted to kiss *him*.

"I..." Her heart pumped a new surge of excitement through her veins. "Would you follow me home?"

His shoulders relaxed. "Sure. Still nervous in the dark?"

"The dark?" Lori stared at him.

Oh. He didn't get it. His expression remained watchful, a little less than casual, but he wasn't presuming. Or if he was, he was presuming on the safe side. The cautious side. He thought she was just asking for an escort home.

Darn him.

She swallowed. "I mean, I want you to follow me home and then...come in."

He stilled. "Lori. You're sure?"

Oh, yes.

Josh must have read that answer on her face, because he smiled, slow and patient and so sexy that she shivered. His smile widened. "I'll be right behind you."

Despite Josh's words, he got hung up in a conversation with a business associate as he gathered his coat to leave the country club. He waved her on ahead, and Lori had gone, glad for a few minutes alone at her apartment before Josh arrived.

She let herself inside, then scurried around, resettling a pillow on her small living-room couch, putting out fresh towels in the bathroom, straightening the comforter on her bed. The bed.

She stared down at it, her face heating as she imagined sharing the double mattress with Josh. He wouldn't fit!

Unless he was really, really close to her.

Lori's breath caught. It wasn't panic, though, but anticipation that closed her throat. She was going to be with Josh. He was the prize at the end of this long road of getting her life back. He was the proof that she was a normal woman again.

He was the man she wanted in her bed. In her life.

Heart fluttering, she walked back to the kitchen. She should offer him something when he arrived. Coffee? Tea? Her hands shook as she filled the kettle and set it on the stove. As she whirled back toward the cupboard that held the teabags, her gaze caught on her answering machine, shoved in the far corner of one counter. The message-waiting light blinked an insistent orange.

She pushed the Play button automatically.

Three replays later, her doorbell rang.

Josh waited outside Lori's door for her to answer his knock, trying to clamp down on the driving need pulsing through his body. She wanted him.

His patience had paid off. By letting her pick the time, the time had arrived much sooner than he'd expected. His heart slammed against his chest as her door slowly opened. It was going to be so good between them.

Then he saw her face. It was pale, so pale, the sapphire blue of her eyes glittering with unshed tears.

His hopes fell to the ground, broke into a hundred pieces. She was afraid again. He took a deep breath, drawing on his well of patience. "Honey," he said, his chest aching with the need to reach out to her. "It's okay. We don't have to—"

"You don't understand," she said, her voice thin.

"I do," he answered. "You're entitled to second thoughts. Third, fourth, whatever you need."

Her head shook from side to side. She pulled the door wide. "Come in and sit down."

Puzzled, Josh obeyed. He took a spot on her couch, then looked up at her, waiting for her next move.

She bit her lip. "Tea? Would you like some tea?"

He didn't want anything but the answer to what was disturbing her. But she looked like she needed something, so he nodded. "Please. Lots of sugar." That's the way he hoped she'd fix hers, too. He wouldn't drink the stuff, but she seemed almost...in shock.

The idea worried the hell out of him.

He didn't feel any better when she came into the living room carrying two steaming mugs. She handed one to him, then took a seat in a small chair across the room. With precise movements, she set down her mug on a small table beside it. Then she frowned at the tea, fussing with its placement, until it sat directly in the center of the tabletop.

Her odd concentration worried Josh even more. "Lori."

She didn't look up.

"Lori. Honey. You need to tell me what's going on."

Her eyes closed. "I should have told you before. I...just couldn't bear to."

Josh's gut clenched. "Tell me now, honey," he said gently.

Her lower lip slid out. "I wish...I wish I didn't have to."

He swallowed. "I know."

Her gaze flicked toward his face, then went back to her mug of tea. "What I told you before, about my ex-husband, well, that wasn't all of it."

"Okay." Josh told himself to take it slow. "What's all of it?"

"I told you how I left him after that second beating."

"Yes." And the hearing of it had nearly pulled his heart out of his chest. There'd been a roaring in his ears then, an anger rising up in him that he had wanted badly to vent. But knowing it would only make her more wary of men, he'd battled it back.

"I went to a motel and immediately called a lawyer, who made me file a police report. I eventually didn't press charges in exchange for David's cooperation during the divorce. That part went surprisingly quickly." She picked up her tea and sipped at it, a tinge of color returning to her cheeks.

"But then he came after you again."

Lori looked up at him, obviously startled. "How did you know?"

Josh hoped he looked calm, though he felt anything but. "An unlucky guess."

She released a breath, and the steam rising from the mug in her hands shifted. "He was waiting for me after work one night. He said he wanted to talk. I knew that wasn't a good idea, but when I tried to get to my car, he…hurt me again."

"He beat you."

Lori straightened her shoulders and met his gaze squarely. "Yes."

"You called the police?"

"I drove to the station immediately afterward. They arrested him. He agreed to an anger-management program."

"But it didn't manage his anger?" Josh heard his own voice, controlled. Cold. He'd never felt such icy coldness.

"No. So I switched jobs, made sure my phone number was unlisted, changed what town I lived in. I did everything I could, Josh, to get away from him. But he kept finding me. Finally I got sick of my fear and moved out-of-state. To Whitehorn."

No wonder she honed her self-defense skills. Her

ex-husband had not only hurt her, but he'd stalked her. *Was* stalking her? Josh heard that roaring in his ears again. "Has he found you here, Lori?" Part of him hoped so. Part of him wanted five minutes, just five minutes with the bastard.

"I don't know. I don't think so." She shrugged. "But when I left, I asked one of our old neighbors in the condo complex to call me if David left town. He was still living there, you see."

"And?"

Her gaze flicked toward the kitchen. "Mrs. Ayers left a message on my machine tonight. David's mailbox is overflowing. There are newspapers piling up outside his door. She hasn't seen him in four days."

"Maybe he's just sick," Josh said.

"Maybe." Lori shrugged again. "But when Mrs. Ayers mentioned the papers and mail to another neighbor, he said David told him he was taking a vacation out west."

Unable to sit still any longer, Josh jumped up from his place on the couch. He paced to the front window, staring into the darkness. "Does he have any idea that you moved here?"

Lori hesitated a moment, then shook her head. "I don't see how he could. Still…"

"You're scared."

"I'm…"

Something in her voice made Josh turn around. "You're…?" he prompted.

She looked at him, her gaze running from his eyes to his feet, and then back. A wave of color rushed up her face. "I'm angry." She blinked, as if her own answer surprised her.

"Angry?"

She nodded. "I'm mad, mad as hell." Her mug hit the little table beside her with an impatient clack. "This is *my* life and I don't want him messing it up again." She rose from her chair and strode toward him.

In the face of all that sudden female determination, Josh froze. Emotions were twisting through him, outrage, protectiveness, worry, but there was a militant light in Lori's eyes that pushed his feelings aside. When she stood, toe-to-toe with him, he looked down into her flushed face and bright eyes.

He read rebellion.

"Lori, I don't know what's going through that beautiful head of yours, but—"

"I want you."

His heart slammed against his chest. Lust surged. "Not as a way to forget," he heard himself saying. Damn, where were all these scruples coming from?

The expression on her face echoed his own mental question. "I wanted you *before* I got the message about David," she said hotly.

There was that, of course. But still… "I want this to be about *us,* Lori. I don't want it to be about you proving something to your ex, or even just to yourself."

Her face softened. "Josh, don't you understand?" She placed the palms of her hands on his chest. "If it wasn't you, if there wasn't an us, I wouldn't be this far."

He groaned. "Lori—"

"I don't want anything to ruin our plans for the evening." She slid her palms upward to link her hands behind his head. With one tug they were mouth-to-mouth. "Don't let him take something from me again."

Once more, anger flamed inside Josh. The SOB had taken from her. Stalked her. Scared her. *Hurt her.* It took every ounce of willpower he had to tamp down the fires of rage. She didn't need that now.

And the truth was, he needed something even more. With a slow, deliberate movement, he placed his hands on the curves of her hips. Lightly, without possession.

She swayed toward him. "Please, Josh."

He bent his head. "Please, Lori," he echoed, "let me please you."

Chapter Nine

Josh's touch, warm and gentle, caused Lori's heartbeat to pound even as her stomach clenched in nervousness. As much as she wanted to be with him, she worried that her fears might get in the way.

But she wouldn't let that happen. She wouldn't! Retreating wouldn't be fair to Josh, not when they'd come this far.

She lifted her mouth and touched her lips to his. He was big, so big, but he was *Josh*. She only had to focus on that.

He lifted his head, a half-smile on his gorgeous mouth. The corners of his eyes tilted up in good humor too, but the irises were dark, darker than she'd ever seen them. She suppressed a shiver.

Josh lightly palmed her hips. ''How are we going to do this?''

Lori swallowed. "Don't you know?"

"Aren't you funny." His lips twitched and he tapped her nose with one long finger. "'Course I know how. But I also know I make you nervous."

Lori wished she could deny it. "I'll be fine."

Josh smiled, that slow, patient one that had won her over from the very start. The one that, if she told the truth, also made her burn. "I'm counting on it." His voice lowered. "So dance me to your bedroom, honey."

"Dance?"

"I don't think I want to let you go, not even for a minute. So dance me there."

What could she say in the face of all that charm? Lori found herself smiling, and walking backward, too, toward the short hallway. "I've never been danced to bed before."

"Cha-cha-cha." Josh wiggled his eyebrows.

Lori was laughing as she crossed the threshold to her bedroom. Then Josh's gaze moved past her and his face changed, its masculine lines hardening. Her laughter died and she glanced behind her, seeing what Josh did—the dim room, the wide bed with its comforter turned back, the satin scalloped edge of one pillowcase gleaming in the soft light from the bedside lamp.

"I'm making you nervous again."

Lori's gaze jumped back to Josh. His expression was rueful. "No, I—" She shrugged, rueful herself. "Yes."

"I *am* still a man, Lori."

Oh, she'd never doubted that. Not with his heavy shoulders beneath her hands and his brawny thigh muscles brushing against hers. She had to smile. "That's what I like best about you."

"Tease." Josh leaned down to touch his lips to hers, his mouth serious, the kiss deep.

Lori parted her lips and he brushed his tongue across the lower one. She heard herself moan. It was an unconscious invitation, so needy-sounding she surprised herself.

Josh lifted his head. "Lori," he whispered. His eyes searched her face and then he lowered his mouth to hers again. His tongue swept across her lips once more, then swept inside her mouth. The kiss swept her away.

His tongue was hot and smooth and it slid against hers. Her fingers dug into his shoulders, the wide maleness of them not so frightening as substantial, something worth holding on to as ripples of reaction skittered across her skin. She sank into the sensation, she let herself drown in the heat he was building inside her, she drifted deeper so that her fears couldn't find her.

His tongue retreated, then pressed into her mouth again, more insistent. She crowded up against him, her tightening nipples needing contact. His touch still light on her hips, he urged her closer with his palms. She breathed in Josh-scent, green and clean and good. So good.

His hands drew her even nearer. She went on tiptoe, rubbing herself against his hard chest.

Josh shuddered.

Lori froze.

He must have felt the new stiffness in her body, because he broke off the kiss, groaning. "Lori," he said hoarsely. "I'm sorry, honey. I'm so damn clumsy. I didn't mean to—"

"Shh," Lori said fiercely. "Shh." She looked into his face and read the concern there…and verified something else.

Josh was scared too.

Oh, not in the same ways that she was, of course, but he was definitely operating at less-than-full confidence. To see big, oh-so-male Josh at the mercy of anxiety—or, well, maybe her?—quieted her own nagging nerves.

Sapped them of their power. She smiled at him.

"God, you're beautiful," he whispered. "I want you, Lori."

She rubbed her knuckles against the stubble along his jaw. "Then take me," she said.

He shook his head. "No." Then he dropped his hands from her, stepped away.

Lori's eyes widened. To have come this far and— "No?" she echoed.

He crossed his arms over his chest. "I think you'll feel more comfortable if you're in control, honey."

Lori swallowed. "In control how?"

"You tell me when to touch. How to touch. Where to touch."

Her skin tingled. "Oh, no—"

"Oh, yes." He took another step away until his

hips found the edge of her dresser. Leaning against it, he crossed his feet at the ankles. Then he nodded at her. "So go ahead and undress."

A wave of heat washed over Lori's skin. An excited hum started buzzing in her ears. "I—" Then she narrowed her eyes. "You just gave me an order. That's not me in control."

His lips twitching, he shrugged.

"*You* undress," Lori said.

Josh opened his mouth. Closed it. His fingers moved to the top button of his shirt.

Lori's heartbeat thrummed against her breastbone. Her skin felt tight. Josh unbuttoned his shirt, pulled the tails out of his pants, then casually tossed it aside.

Lori's mouth dried as she silently cursed winter. Surely if this was summer, she wouldn't have had to wait so long to see Josh's naked chest. Even now she could imagine him in nothing but low-slung Levis and a tool belt, sweat rolling over his strong pec muscles.

One of his eyebrows winged up. "Like what you see?"

She nodded dumbly.

"What next?" he asked.

Lori had to swallow to get the words out. "I want to…to touch you."

He lifted his arms from his sides, a casual gesture, though she saw his nostrils flare. "I'm not stopping you."

The thrill of power licked through her as she approached him. He didn't move as she drew closer, maybe he didn't even breathe. When they were just an inch apart, she halted. His body heat radiated toward her and she breathed in another dizzying gulp of Josh's scent.

Her hands lifted to the buttons of her blouse.

If Josh *had* been breathing, he certainly wasn't now. His voice was strained. "I thought—I thought you wanted to touch me," he said.

"I do," she answered. She slid her blouse off her shoulders and it fell silently to the carpet. "I want to touch you like this." She closed the last inch between their bodies.

His skin burned her, even through the lace of her bra. She gasped, her nipples contracting to even tighter, more sensitive points. "Josh…"

His head was tilted back, his eyes were closed. "Good," he said. "You feel so good."

Once again, the impact she could clearly see she had on him freed her. Curling her arms around his neck, she snuggled closer to Josh, rubbing the lacy cups against his chest. "You feel good too." She kissed his chin.

He groaned.

The sound only bolstered her confidence. It only made her want him more, this big, sexy man who was letting her take her time, who was letting her make all the moves. Desire sped through her body, and without a second thought she reached behind her back and unhooked her bra. With a little shimmy, the straps slipped from her shoulders, the cups slid off her breasts.

Her naked nipples met his naked skin.

They groaned together, then the sound was muffled as their mouths met too. Josh controlled the kiss, took it hot and deep, but Lori reveled in it, because he was under her control too. The truth of that was in every one of his ragged breaths, in the tension in his hard muscles, in the sound he made, low and hardly contained, when she drew one hand over his chest and found the stiff point of his own nipple.

He tore his mouth away from hers. "You're killing me," he said.

She pressed her lips against his heart, feeling it pounding quick and sure. "You seem all right to me." She kissed across to one nipple, felt compelled to taste it with her tongue.

"Lori…" He groaned again. "I'm trying to let you have your way, but…"

Her tongue slid across that delicious point again.

"…it's hard."

She suppressed a giggle as she tilted her hips into his. "I know."

"Very funny," he said, but he wasn't laughing.

And then Lori wasn't either. The rigid feel of Josh against her, that hard part of him against her belly, turned the heat up another notch on her simmering desire. Places inside her began aching with an insistent throb.

Startled by the rapid escalation of passion, she looked up, into Josh's eyes.

Almost black, they gazed back down at her. "Feel it, honey?" he whispered.

She nodded.

With a slow movement, he fisted one hand in the back of her hair and drew her head back farther. His mouth slid across her mouth, she tried to catch it with her own, but he kept moving, over her chin, down her neck.

"Peaches," he murmured. Kisses burned across her throat, down the slope of one breast. Then his mouth latched onto her nipple and sucked, strong and hot.

Lori gasped. Her knees buckled and she gripped the sleek, heated skin of Josh's shoulders to stay on her feet. The throbbing inside her redoubled, demanding now, as he tasted her other nipple.

She hadn't known anything could be this good. Josh's strength, his heat, were focused on her, feeding her desire. His size only made him more beautiful, more to touch, more to appreciate, more to explore.

Her fingers slid down his arms to the button of his jeans. Josh froze, his face buried between her breasts. Lori swallowed. "I'm in control here, remember?" she whispered. "This next."

A breath shuddered into Josh's lungs. "Whatever you say." He backed away from her, standing straight again.

His dark eyes trained on her face, Lori lost her nerve. Her fingers fumbled at his waistband. He caught her hands, squeezed them between his. "Shall I?"

Lori couldn't look at him, so she nodded, her gaze on their linked fingers. He slowly released her and made swift work of the button and zipper. After one brief hesitation, he shoved down his pants, taking a pair of dark boxers with them. Without an apparent care in the world, he took the time to toe off his running shoes too, so that in another moment he was completely naked.

Largely naked.

He was big everywhere, of course, all his maleness proportionate to his size, but it was the entire package that took her breath. Long thick bones covered by heavy muscles covered by sleek skin.

He was a naked, beautiful male animal.

He was Josh.

She couldn't believe how much she wanted him.

"I…" Her hand lifted, fell to her side. She didn't have the words to tell him.

"May I undress you?" he asked.

Undress her? Lori blinked. She'd been so fascinated by him, so entranced, she'd completely forgotten herself. With Josh in the room, with her desire for him, there wasn't room for anything else it seemed. Her hands went to the waistband of her wool slacks. "I can do it."

He touched the back of her hand. "Let me."

Her fingers fell away.

His touch was quick, sure, but she detected the power of his need in the sound of his quick breaths and the caressing way that his knuckles slid along her belly as he pushed the rest of her clothing away. In moments, they faced each other, both naked, their chests rising and falling as if they'd been running.

He swallowed. "You're…more than I dreamed."

Lori didn't think she could talk. She didn't have the extra air. She didn't have the words to tell him how vulnerable she felt…and yet how strong. "Take me…" She had to wet her lips with her tongue to finish. "Take me to bed, Josh."

Without moving his gaze from her, he took the few steps to the bed. He sat on the edge of the mattress, his long legs in front of him, and lifted his hand to her. "Come here, Lori."

She grasped his hand and let him draw her between his spread knees. Standing above him, she placed her free hand on his silky dark hair, then drew his head toward her breasts. He laid his cheek against her heart and she stroked his hair, knowing he could hear her desire in its rapid beat, knowing he could feel her excitement in the shivers rolling across her skin.

Then he turned his head, caught her nipple between his teeth, and tugged.

Lori moaned, sagged against him, felt herself falling. Josh caught her, sliding back onto the bed so that he lay flat against the mattress and she lay flat against him. His mouth found hers, and the kiss was an explosion of need, desire, lust.

All the tentative moves were over now. All the give-and-take was unchoreographed, unpracticed, just the raw drive to touch, to taste, to know.

In the back of her mind, Lori realized Josh was still taking pains not to cage her or control her, but her mind wasn't so clear. She slid over him, rubbing her palms over his chest, licking the rippled muscles of his abdomen, tasting the underside of his chin.

He caught her, pulling her over him to bring her breasts to his mouth. He held her like that, kissing and sucking, while the lower half of her body draped across the lower half of his. "Josh," she cried, trying to tell him it wasn't enough. "Josh."

He laid her flat against the mattress and her body opened up to him, her thighs parting in invitation, but Josh wasn't done touching. He parted her, caressed her, nearly carried her away. Just as she thought she'd reached it, found what he'd been making her crave, he withdrew his touch.

She grabbed his arm and he laughed, the sound wicked and sweet. "Just a second, honey."

Then he was back, his touch *there* again. He took her up a second time, and just as she started to tremble, he pulled her body over on top of his. He drew up her knees and she half sat on his thighs. "Oh."

Josh's eyelids lowered. "Oh, man."

He'd put on protection and the hard ridge of his body was pressed just where hers throbbed. Where it ached.

"Lift up a little, honey," he said. His hands closed on her hips to encourage her. Then with one hand, he positioned himself right at the wet, hot entrance to her body.

"Now," he said, his voice guttural. "You're in charge."

Lori paused, desire sharpening with every moment she hesitated. Then Josh lifted his hand and brushed his thumb over her nipple. Heat blazed through her body.

In a rush, she slid down on him.

They both gasped.

He was big. So big, that her body tightened around him in near-rejection. She made to move off him, but Josh's palm drifted to her backside. "Relax, honey," he said. "Just give it a minute." His touch was warm and soothing. "Just another minute."

His other hand drew her head down to his, and he kissed her. It was a Josh-kiss, deep and hot, and Lori found herself melting into him. The too-full discomfort receded, and as Josh slid his tongue in and out of her mouth, Lori found her body echoing its movements.

Josh praised her with his mouth and his hands. The next thing she knew, she was riding him, taking him, having her way with him. Desire surged through her the way her body surged against Josh's. There was no longer any control, no longer any power but the power of Josh under her, with her, in her.

His hand insinuated itself between their bodies. He touched her there, and heat blazed through her, tension coiling tight. Lori threw back her head.

"Go, baby," Josh murmured. "And take me with you."

He gave the orders after all, Lori thought, then pleasure buckled her. She fell across Josh's chest as the waves came, and she tasted the salty goodness of his sweat as he pumped his own pleasure into her.

Lori was spread over Josh like a layer of warm honey. He felt the air going in and out of her lungs, slowly, evenly. She was probably asleep, with his body still inside hers.

He closed his eyes on the image, knowing that wasn't the way to make it out from under her. But he had to. He hated disturbing the moment, but there was the practical matter of the condom to deal with.

As gently as he could, he shifted her slack warmth, gritting his teeth as their bodies disengaged. She murmured a little in protest, then buried her head in the pillow beside him. He rolled off the mattress and padded into the adjacent bathroom.

With the door closed so the light wouldn't disturb her, he dispensed with the protection. Then, leaning over the sink, he turned on the cold tap water. He splashed some onto his face, then stared into his own heavy-eyed image in the mirror. Hanging his head, he cupped his hands and gathered more water, splashed it up against his face again, trying to bring back his senses.

His common sense.

Because somewhere between "this is your temporary receptionist" and "I want you, Josh," he'd come to care about Lori deeply. He could no longer fool himself that being with her was some kind of Samaritan impulse. Inhaling a long breath, he turned off the tap. Then he turned out the light and reentered the bedroom.

She was asleep, this woman he cared for so much. The outside edge of the small arc of meager light from the lamp at her bedside just reached her face, turned in profile against the white pillow. His heart jolted in his chest at its beauty, its serenity. Something primitive blossomed inside him at the same time. It was his lovemaking that had brought her that peace.

She stirred, her eyes opened sleepily. "Josh?" she murmured.

"Right here." He approached the bed, swooping down for his boxers and slipping them on before taking a seat on the edge of the mattress. She blinked up at him and he reached out to push her hair off her cheek and tuck it behind her ear.

"You're too far away," she said.

He smiled, though still hesitating. Lori had trusted him with her body, but how far did she really want to take their intimacy? As for himself...maybe he needed distance too, maybe with a little distance he would realize he hadn't made such a risky leap of the heart.

"Josh?" She lifted one arm. "I'm cold."

It was as simple as that, of course. He slid under the covers. Still leery of frightening her, he forced himself not to reach for her and instead let her scoot across the inches of mattress to align their bodies.

She sighed, a contented sound.

He sighed too, soundless though, afraid of giving too much away. Her cheek pillowed against his arm, she slept.

Josh guarded that sleep. Now, with his desire for her temporarily sated, he watched over her and remembered everything that had happened that night. Not just the explosive combination of their bodies, but what she'd told him when he'd arrived at her door.

She thought her ex-husband might be stalking her.

God. The idea was enough never to let him sleep again.

Or never to let her sleep alone again.

Closing his eyes, he stroked a finger down her bare shoulder, unable to stop himself. There wasn't one instant of the evening he wanted to take back, but he needed time to take it all in, time to fully assess the changes that had just come over his life.

"Josh?"

He opened his eyes. Lori was looking at him, a frown line between her arched black brows. His smile felt forced, but he tried it out anyway, hating that worry on her face. "Shh, honey. Go to sleep."

Her hand pushed his hair off his forehead. "Are you all right?"

He reached for her fingers and brought them to his lips. "You amazed me."

Her face softened. "Because you made it so easy for me to…to be with you."

He smiled, this one easier. "I'm glad."

"But now you're worried about something."

Guess that left him out of the running for an Academy Award, he thought, sighing inwardly. Still, he wasn't going to burden her, not tonight. "I'm bowled over." That was the truth, anyway.

She bit her bottom lip. "As flattered as I am, Josh, I think there's more going on inside your head."

"You flatter *me*," he said, trying to distract her.

"A man like me, there's not a whole lot going on inside my head after holding you in my arms."

"It's David."

Josh hesitated. "It's hard to forget," he finally admitted.

Lori's gaze searched his face. "I understand. But I truly can't see how he'd know to come to Whitehorn."

Still, Josh felt his muscles tighten. It took all his force of will not to haul her up against him. Instead, he contented himself with sliding his palm down her shoulder. "But if he does, I won't let him hurt you."

Her gaze slid away from his face. "That's not your job, Josh."

The words were a warning to him, he knew that immediately, but they couldn't ease his need to protect her. "Job or not—"

"No, Josh. I'm not hiding behind you. That's not why I'm with you."

There was steel in her soft Southern voice. But there was steel in Josh, too. "I didn't say that's why you're with me, Lori. But I—"

She put her hand over his mouth. "Let's not talk about this now, Josh. Please."

He pulled back on the reins of his mood. The lady didn't want to talk about her ex-husband when she was in bed with him. In bed with him for the very first time. Hell, and he wanted to complain about that?

But, if he didn't care for her so damn much, this would be infinitely easier.

As if she sensed his capitulation, she smiled at him

and snuggled closer. "Now go to sleep," she said. "You're going to need your energy later."

He lifted a brow. "I am?"

"Mmm." Her eyes drifted closed. "Because you're going to get lucky."

"Lucky?" There wasn't a worry that could tarnish the shining promise of that. He shifted closer to her and rested his chin on the top of her head, breathing in the scent of peaches. "I already am, sweetheart."

Chapter Ten

The following Saturday, Josh and Lori approached the front entrance to the Whitehorn Country Club. She looked up at him, her happy smile warming the brisk winter air.

"New Year's Eve, the bridal shower, now a wedding reception," she said, her Southern accent stretching every syllable. "I'm beginning to feel quite the regular here."

Josh couldn't stop himself from reaching out to lightly stroke her long fall of dark hair. She didn't flinch, and he savored the moment, just as he'd been savoring each one since they'd made love a few nights before. Though they hadn't shared a bed since—once again he was waiting for her to initiate the event—each day she relaxed around him more.

For himself, he'd been able to relax some as well. One night of passion didn't have to mean an irrevocable change to his life.

"Whitehorn doesn't take long to make you one of its own," he said.

Shaking her head, Lori paused and put her hand on his forearm. "No, Josh. It's thanks to you. I know that. You're the one who introduced me to your friends. You're the one who invited me as your date to the wedding today."

"You would have received your own invitation, except Darcy and Mark know we're a couple."

A teasing smile played over her mouth. "Is that what we are, then? A couple?"

Josh swallowed, treading carefully now. There was a whole laundry list of things they hadn't talked about. How lovemaking had changed their relationship. What they were to each other now. Where they went from here. What to do about the potential threat of her ex-husband.

Every time he thought of that damn threat, despite his vow to take this slow, a primitive need drove Josh to want to bind Lori to him, to claim her as his own. Taking a breath, he clamped down on the impulse for the hundredth time.

"Close enough to a couple," he made himself respond lightly.

They had just attended Darcy and Mark's wedding, and now they were headed to the reception. It was a time for celebration, and he didn't want anything— including serious conversation—to mar the occasion.

Lori seemed to read his mind. She smiled again, a carefree smile that lightened the day like a burst of sunshine, and he touched her cheek and then the small of her back as he urged her toward the door.

Her peachy scent drifted up to him as he held it open, and he sniffed with appreciation before taking the first step to follow her in. "Mmm. Did I tell you that you smell de—"

"Hold the door, Josh!" an exuberant voice sang out behind him.

Lori kept walking as Josh paused and looked over his shoulder. Another Whitehorn resident, Connie Adams, was hurrying toward him, the sides of her open coat flapping in her haste. He gave the forty-something woman a polite smile. "Good afternoon," he said.

"I'm looking for Wyatt," Connie answered. "Have you seen him?"

"No—" Josh started.

"You must have. I'm sure it was Melissa who just walked inside."

Josh frowned, looking into the restaurant. "Melissa?" As he said the name, Lori apparently noticed he wasn't right behind her and she turned, backtracking toward him. "Ah. Not Melissa. That was Lori. Is Lori." As she reached him, her head tilted in mild inquiry, he made the introductions.

Connie's eyes narrowed, and she raked her fingernails through her ash-blond hair. "You look like Melissa," she said, her tone almost accusing.

Lori blinked. "Well, um…"

Connie swept past them, no longer interested. "I have to find Wyatt," she said.

As the other woman moved away, Josh met Lori's gaze, then shrugged. "I think she's been spending a little too much time with our town eccentric, Homer Gilmore. Connie's a nurse and has been taking care of him."

"Ah." Lori nodded. "I think I saw her wandering around downtown the other day with an elderly man. Does Homer have long gray hair? Wears a bathrobe and slippers?"

"That's him." The distinctive sound of a cork being released reached his ears and he laced his fingers with Lori's. "Come on. That champagne is calling my name."

"Your name is Pop? And here I've been calling you Josh all along." She grinned.

"Aren't you the jokester?" Then he smiled, pleased at her cheery mood. He slanted her a glance, then slowed his footsteps. "You know, Connie's right. You *do* look like Melissa."

"Must be more of Whitehorn rubbing off on me," Lori said.

Before he could answer, they ran into the end of the line of guests waiting to sign the guestbook. After their turn with the feather-topped pen, they were directed to find their places at one of the round tables in the room. Bless Darcy's heart, because their place-cards were at the table where the Norths were seated, as well as Mark's sister Maddie and other good friends of Josh's that Lori had met on New Year's Eve or at the bridal shower.

If he couldn't wrap her in his protection, he could at least wrap her up in Whitehorn friendship.

Just as they seated themselves, Wyatt slipped into the empty chair beside Melissa's, handing her the glass of cola he'd apparently retrieved for her at the bar on one side of the room. "You were supposed to rescue me," he muttered.

"What?" Melissa's eyes rounded in innocence.

"You know what I mean," Wyatt grumbled.

Josh reached over Lori's head to grab a couple of glasses of champagne from a passing waiter. "What's going on, you two?" he asked, handing one glass to Lori.

"There's a tenet of marriage that my wife appears to have conveniently forgotten," Wyatt said.

"What tenet is that?" Maddie asked. "Not that I have plans on getting married anytime soon, but I like to be prepared."

Josh leaned toward Lori. "Maddie is a champion barrel racer. She travels all over the country competing in rodeos. I can't imagine her settling down in one place, let alone settling for one man."

Maddie wrinkled her nose at him. "You be quiet, Josh Anderson. My brother got married today and there isn't anything he can do that I can't do too." She turned her attention back to Wyatt. "So what is it that Melissa forgot?"

"It's one of the unspoken vows between husband

and wife," Wyatt said. "'Thou shalt rescue thy spouse from awkward situations.'"

Melissa sipped her champagne and smiled serenely. "Wyatt, my love, I rescued you from an awkward bachelorhood by marrying you. What more do you want?"

Everyone at the table laughed, Wyatt too, though he shook a teasing finger at his wife. "What you were *supposed* to do is rescue me from Connie Adams," he said. "She cornered me while I was standing in line at the bar."

Melissa waved her hand. "I freely admit it. I escaped, leaving you with her because I wasn't in the mood to hear more complaints about the Hip Hop's food."

"She doesn't like the food?" Josh asked. "I've seen her eat there dozens of times."

"No, no," Melissa replied. "*She* likes the food all right. It's Homer who says we've been trying to poison him. For some reason Connie feels compelled to pass on every one of Homer's nutty gripes."

Maddie frowned. "Does Mark know this? Isn't he in charge of the Hip Hop's arson investigation? Maybe Homer—"

"It wasn't about the Hip Hop," Wyatt said. "Connie wanted me to promise to dance with her once the music starts."

"Oh." Melissa threw Wyatt a sympathetic look. "I'm sorry. That *was* awkward for you. What did you say?"

"That I save all my dances for you," he answered, wearing a patently adoring expression.

"*Aaaaah*," the other occupants of the table cried as one, then burst into laughter.

Melissa tilted her nose in the air. "Go ahead and laugh all of you without romantic bones in your bodies, but I *do* adore this man. It's not every husband who would save all his dances and thus all the broken toes just for me."

As the people around the table laughed again, Josh watched Melissa soften her teasing by leaning toward Wyatt and giving him a long, warm kiss on the mouth. Wyatt lifted his hand and touched his wife's face, as if he still couldn't believe that her beauty and her love belonged to him.

Josh glanced at Lori. Her gaze was on the married couple too, a faint smile curving her lips. His heart slammed against his chest.

What Melissa and Wyatt had, he wanted too.

That same laughter, that same ease and confidence in the relationship. The partnership of marriage that he'd never achieved with Kay, either because they were too young or because she'd never let him get that close.

He noticed that Lori was looking at him now, her expression slightly puzzled. "Are you okay?" she asked.

A sudden chill edged down his spine and he shook it off. "I'm fine. Fine." He lifted his champagne glass and touched it to hers. "To..."

He couldn't think what kind of toast to make.

Her eyebrows rose.

''To today,'' Josh said firmly, because that was all he was going to ask for at the moment.

It seemed like enough. As the band started to play and the lids were lifted on the chafing dishes at the buffet table, Josh thought he could live forever on good music, good food, the company of good friends. With Lori by his side. Her soft Southern voice, her soft peachy scent, the promise that he would be able to sink into her soft body sometime soon.

As the afternoon wore on, Josh's good mood only escalated. He leaned back in his chair, not joining in the conversation, but instead watching Lori, her face animated and trusting. Her shyness was almost completely gone now, and he half listened as she plied Maddie Kincaid with questions about her life on the rodeo circuit.

This was the real Lori, he thought. The one who approached life with smiles and self-confident assurance. He promised himself to nurture this Lori, not to push her too hard or hold her too tightly. With more time in the security of Whitehorn, she'd come to him of her own accord, she'd embrace them as a couple instead of teasing about it.

He could wait for that.

He *would* wait for that.

A collective gasp went up around the table and he straightened, tuning back into the conversation. Maddie was cataloging the injuries she'd suffered over the years as a barrel racer. Melissa shook her head. ''I don't see how you can be so stoic about that, Maddie.

I don't like to break a fingernail, let alone bruise my ribs.''

Maddie grinned. ''That's because you're such a girly-girl, Melissa. My brother Mark and my Aunt June raised me to be tough….''

At that, war stories about scrapes, bruises and broken bones were swapped around the table. Wyatt regaled them with details of a fractured ankle, Lori had once broken her arm and collarbone. Melissa, of course, complained of a particularly disastrous manicure mishap. The talk continued and Josh lazed farther back in his chair, grinning to himself. All's right with the world, he thought, lifting his champagne glass. His mind drifted again.

''…they wired it shut.''

Josh caught the tail end of Lori's words and saw Melissa shudder with a sympathetic wince. His fingers tightened on the stem of his glass. ''What?''

Even Maddie looked a little green. ''Lori was telling us what the doctors did when she broke her jaw,'' she murmured.

When she broke her jaw. When she broke her collarbone. When she broke her arm. He'd dismissed the latter two as childhood injuries, but now he guessed he'd been wrong.

Her ex-husband had done those things to her.

Josh stilled, something inside his chest going as hard and cold as Montana earth in winter. Then that frozen place cracked open, and heat spilled out, liquid and burning to fill his body. His soul. He jumped to his feet, his chair falling backward, hitting the parquet floor with a crash.

"Josh?" Lori's eyes rounded. The rest of the table looked at him as if he were crazy too.

"We have to go," he said.

Lori blinked. "What?"

He didn't have an explanation, at least one he could make in front of the entire table. Hell, he didn't have one he felt comfortable telling *her*.

"Are you sick?" Melissa asked, starting to rise.

Josh laughed, the sound harsh. "No, no." He waved Melissa back down. "I...I..." He reached out to Lori.

"Of course," she said, coming to her feet. She put her warm hand in his. "If you want to go, we'll go."

She was puzzled of course, but willing. He saw her exchange a concerned look with Melissa. He wanted to kick himself. There was no reason to leave. No reason other than he couldn't stand the idea of someone hurting her.

The idea—the idea of those broken bones—rose like bile in his throat. He closed his eyes, trying to find his breath. "Lori," he said hoarsely.

She squeezed his hand. "We'll go, Josh. Maybe you'll feel better outside."

He opened his eyes. "No, no. I'm better now." It was a hell of a lie, but he couldn't take her away. He shouldn't. She was having fun and he was going to have to live with...whatever this was that was going on inside him.

Rage at what had happened to her. Fear that something might happen to her again. And...

Love.

God help him, there was no use pretending it wasn't true any longer. He was in love with her.

She was staring at him with those eyes of hers, honest and blue. It was all he could do not to haul her up against him and whisper—hell, shout!—what she meant to him. What she'd done to him.

Josh Anderson, who had thought he'd had his one chance at love, had fallen once more. Fallen harder, fallen deeper than he'd ever thought possible.

Josh Anderson—who'd thought he was smarter than that—had fallen in love with a woman who could break his heart once and for all. Forever.

"Dance with me," he said hoarsely.

She hesitated. He remembered New Year's Eve, when she'd been leery of being in his arms. But he had to touch her, hold her. After another moment, she nodded.

He led her to the dance floor, hoping like hell he could keep the truth his secret.

Lori moved into Josh's arms, letting him pull her close. Still concerned, she looked up. "Are you sure you're all right?"

His face was tense and unsmiling, not a Josh kind of expression at all. "I'm fine," he answered. "And you...is it okay if I hold you like this?"

His arms enclosed her, but Lori was so worried about him that she hadn't even noticed. She nodded, realizing it *was* okay. Very okay. With a sigh, she rested her head against his wide chest and let herself savor the sensation of being held.

His shoulders rose and fell slowly, as if he were inhaling his first full breath in a long while. He lowered his head and leaned his cheek against hers. "Lori?"

"Hmm?"

"This is good, isn't it?"

Lori closed her eyes. "Oh, it's very good."

"We're good."

"Yes." Lori couldn't deny it. Didn't want to. Josh—his touch, his humor, his patience—was mending her. Healing her. Making her feel normal again. When they'd made love the other night, it had been a balm to her soul. They hadn't made love since, and she appreciated Josh's patience even more, but they *would* make love again. She wanted to. She wanted him.

"You're enjoying yourself today?" he asked.

"You know I am. I hoped it could be…like this." She lifted her head to look into his dark eyes. "I wanted to find a place in the community. I wanted to find…friends." She'd wanted to find her sister, and that had turned out even better than she thought because Melissa was turning into a friend, too. "I just never expected it to happen so quickly."

He nodded. "Very, very quickly."

She frowned for a moment, not sure if he was talking about the same thing that she was. "It's really happened, though, right? I'm not just imagining it?"

He shook his head. "It's true. All of it. You've made a place for yourself, Lori." He hesitated. "In my heart, too."

She smiled at him, delighted with the sentiment. "You are the sweetest man," she said.

He sighed, his smile rueful. "There you go again. Cute. Nice. Sweet."

"I keep telling you those are the best kind of compliments," she said lightly. "I've had my share of dangerous you know, Josh."

His expression shifted, his half-smile turning strained. "Yes. Well." He lifted his hand and put it on the back of her head, tucking her cheek against his chest once more. "Tell me what you hoped for when you came to Whitehorn."

His heart was beating steadily against her ear. "I told you. A place. Friends."

"What about family?"

She froze for a minute, but then Josh continued. "Did you see yourself raising kids here?" he asked.

Lori closed her eyes. "I'm not sure I ever got that far," she said. But the idea rose in her mind now. Marriage, children, a small town and wide-open spaces. They would grow up western kids, with horses. Unless they were like Josh, of course, and didn't like riding the big beasts.

Like Josh? Lori hastily pulled herself up short. Where had that come from? Had she really made the instant leap from kids to *Josh's* kids?

A little boy with Josh's shaggy hair and patient

grin. A little girl with long pigtails and his dark, intense eyes.

She banished their images, impatient with herself. What gave her the right to imagine his—their—children? It was enough to be here, today, in the company of her half sister and in Josh's arms.

Except...

She swallowed, then lifted her head to meet Josh's gaze. "It could all happen, couldn't it?" she found herself saying.

He didn't ask her what "all" was. Instead, he smiled at her, melting her fears, her knees, her heart. "Yeah," he said, his voice soft but sure. "You could have it all, honey. We could."

We could. Lori's heart seemed to leap, then twirl. There was every reason to dance, she thought dizzily. The possibilities were endless, the potential for happiness not around the corner, but right here. Right now.

She smiled at Josh. He smiled back. His mouth opened. "Lori, I—"

"A doctor! We need a doctor!" The anxious shout had them turning.

Wyatt was standing beside their table, Melissa in his arms. Her face was white and she didn't look as if she was breathing. "For God's sake," Wyatt shouted again, his voice full of fear. "Call an ambulance!"

On Sunday, the day after the wedding, Lori's hands were shaking as she pushed open the door to Melissa's room at the Whitehorn Memorial Hospital. Under the white hospital blanket, Melissa lay still and quiet, but Wyatt looked up from his chair beside the bed, his face lined with exhaustion.

Lori swallowed, then spoke, keeping her voice low. "Hi, Wyatt. The nurse said it was okay to visit."

He gestured her in, though his gaze turned immediately to his wife. "I think she's sleeping."

A wan smile turned up Melissa's pale mouth. "She isn't sleeping, she's just too tired to open her eyes."

Relief coursed through Lori at the sound of her sister's voice. "Maybe I should come back later."

Melissa's hair slid against the white pillow as she slowly shook her head. "No, Lori. Stay. I'm glad you're here. You can give Wyatt a break from his hovering."

Wyatt frowned. "You make me sound like a helicopter."

Melissa opened her eyes, her gaze full of love as she looked on her husband's face. "But a handsome one. Go find some coffee, darling. Then a doctor. I know you've been dying to badger one all morning."

Wyatt touched Melissa's cheek. "First a helicopter, now a badger. I'm not flattered." But he smiled at her.

"I'll flatter you when you get me sent home," Melissa said. "Go find out when you can break me loose from this place."

"Not until I'm certain you're truly on the mend."

Melissa's hand came off the bed, then fell back

against it as if a gesture took too much energy. "It's just the flu."

Wyatt shook his head, but he didn't contradict his wife. Instead, he looked over at Lori. "I *could* use a cup of coffee. And a chance to badger the doctors, as she said. Will you sit with her awhile?"

Lori nodded and came toward the bed. "I'd be happy to." She slipped into Wyatt's chair as he went out the door, setting the small pot of pansies she'd brought onto the table beside Melissa's bed. She leaned close to the other woman. "When you're feeling better, I'll bring candy."

Melissa smiled. "I'd appreciate that. I'm so mad I missed out on the wedding cake. Darcy said it was chocolate inside, and I love chocolate."

Lori shrugged. "I didn't eat any myself. Josh and I left right after the ambulance took you to the hospital."

A frown appeared between Melissa's blue eyes. "Oh, I hope I didn't ruin the reception. I made Wyatt call right away to let everyone know that I was going to be fine."

"I heard the reception went on as planned, a bit subdued, but the party perked back up after Wyatt called. So don't worry."

Melissa pinned Lori with her gaze. "But you did."

Lori didn't know what to say to that. How could she logically explain to Melissa how scared she'd been without also telling her she was her sister? Now certainly wasn't the time for a revelation of those proportions. She swallowed. "Josh was ready to leave, too."

"That's right." Melissa frowned again. "I remember he was acting kind of…odd before I got sick."

"I thought maybe he didn't feel well too, but he says not." Lori thought back, trying to get a bead on Josh's mood of the day before.

"But for the most part you seemed to be having fun at the wedding, right?"

Lori nodded. "A lot of fun." Now that she saw for herself that Melissa was all right, yesterday's sense of well-being resurged inside her. "Everyone has been so kind to me."

"We like you," Melissa said. "I like you."

Lori stilled. "Thank you." She slid her gaze off Melissa's face and trained it on the dark hearts of the pansies, afraid of giving too much away. But her mood lightened even more. Thank God she'd come to Whitehorn! Thank God she'd met Melissa!

The door suddenly swung open. His face a mask of cold determination, Wyatt stalked in, followed by another man who was wearing a white coat. His hospital badge read "Dr. Noah Martin."

Lori's heart jumped. "What's the matter?" Without thinking, she grabbed Melissa's hand. Her sister's fingers were cold, and Lori squeezed them reassuringly, despite the sick fear growing inside her stomach.

Wyatt sat on the mattress on the other side of Melissa. Though his expression was grim, he brushed back the hair on her forehead with a tender touch. "Melissa, Noah got the test results back."

Melissa's gaze moved to the doctor. "What is it?"

He cleared his throat. "You're going to be fine, Melissa, just as I said last night. Still, this is a hell of a thing to have to tell someone."

Lori's stomach clenched. *"What is it?"* She didn't even realize she'd spoken until Wyatt shot her a considering look.

"Go ahead, Noah," Melissa said.

He shoved his hands in the pockets of his coat. "You were poisoned, Melissa. Probably with something you ate or drank at the wedding."

Chapter Eleven

Lori drove straight from the hospital to the gym. After grabbing her bag from the trunk of her car, she hurried inside. The zone, she thought. She needed to get away from all that was pressing on her mind and get into the zone.

The high-school boy at the desk smiled at her as he always did, holding on to her membership card as he copied her number into the ledger book. "You'd think we'd keep track of this on a computer," he said, shaking his head. "I need to talk to my boss about that."

Boss. The word made Lori think of Josh, and she swallowed, wanting to banish him from her mind as well. When he'd taken her home from the wedding last night, he'd asked about her plans for the next day.

She'd hemmed and hawed, purposely not telling him about her inner vow to check in on Melissa. Purposely not giving him an opportunity to suggest they visit the hospital—or do anything else—together.

The boy returned her card, and Lori gave him a brief smile before moving toward the women's locker room to change into her workout clothes. But there wasn't any peace to be found there. As she turned the corner to a bank of lockers, her gaze met another's— one of the young women who had attended Darcy's bridal shower. Lori had exchanged pleasantries with her at the wedding and reception the day before, too.

"Have you heard anything?" the other woman asked immediately. She was dressed in street clothes and she zipped up her bag as if she'd already completed her workout.

Lori hesitated. "Heard anything about what?"

"Who," the woman corrected. "Melissa." She slung the handle of her bag over her shoulder. "She's a special friend of yours, isn't she?"

"Yes. I—I guess she is."

"They announced at the reception that they'd stabilized her, of course, but I wondered if you had an update on how she's feeling."

"I just came from the hospital." In the face of such sincere concern, Lori half smiled. "She says she's tired, but on the mend. She even mentioned chocolate."

The other woman's face relaxed into a smile. "Oh. That's all right then. Talking about chocolate means she's definitely feeling better. Thanks." She walked toward the locker-room door, then paused before exiting. "Maybe we can work out together some time," she said, looking over her shoulder. "I run too."

"Oh. Yes. Sure." Lori replied, surprised by the friendly yet unexpected offer.

The woman smiled again and was gone, leaving Lori staring after her. Whitehorn had done it again—floored her with its small-town camaraderie and easygoing kindliness.

It frightened her too, though.

She stripped quickly and hastened into her sweatshorts, T-shirt and running shoes. Just another few minutes, a few stretches, and she could seek out the zone. Seek out respite from thoughts of Melissa, Josh and even the cordial young woman who had just put out the first feelers of friendship.

Lori closed her eyes, suddenly dismayed by the idea that she wanted to run away from the very things she'd come to Whitehorn to find.

But she wasn't sure it was safe to look for those things here anymore.

With the gray track beneath her feet, Lori took off running after only an abbreviated version of her usual stretching routine. The mural-painted walls blurred, their colors flowing together as they always did, but Lori's mind didn't blur with them.

Instead, as clear as glass, she saw Melissa's pale face. Josh's rugged features, etched with concern. The tentative smile of the woman in the locker room.

What if David found Lori here in Whitehorn and hurt them?

Though there didn't seem to be any possible correlation between Melissa's poisoning and Lori's "gone west" ex-husband, that didn't stop the idea of him harming Melissa from rearing its terrifying head. In the logical, sensible part of her brain, she *knew* that David wasn't responsible. But as sick as it sounded, she wouldn't put such an action past him.

Though it shamed her to think that she'd been married to a man she could have such despicable suspicions about, her shame had never stopped David's anger. What if he decided to direct his animosity at people she cared about, instead of at Lori herself?

Her heart chilled. Until she knew for sure where David was, she needed to be careful. Not for herself, but for Melissa and Josh. If her ex-husband did arrive in town, she wasn't going to let him guess that anyone cared about her.

Or that she cared for anyone.

By Monday afternoon, Josh was ready to tear something apart with his bare hands. Lori had appeared in the office this morning, her mood subdued. With her hair pulled back in a severe braid and wearing black pants and a black blouse buttoned up to the throat, it was obvious she'd retreated inside herself again. It was as if the past weeks had never happened.

It was as if they'd never laughed together.

Loved together.

That maddening, peachy scent of hers swirling around his head, he stared at a set of blueprints spread across his desk. "Lori!" he barked out.

Her eyebrows arched in mild surprise, she appeared in his doorway. "Yes? Did you want something?"

He didn't want anything but to see her, touch her, talk with her. "You never told me how the rest of your weekend was."

She'd resisted every attempt he'd made at conversation from the moment she'd arrived in the office. When he'd called her last night, she'd been polite, but distant then too.

"The rest of my weekend was fine."

He ground his back teeth. "You felt okay? I wondered if Melissa was just the first of a Whitehorn flu epidemic, and you two are pretty tight."

Lori hesitated. "I...No, I don't think I'm catching the flu."

"Well, I had a fine Sunday too." Though she didn't seem the least bit interested in it. "I came into the office and worked." Only because he couldn't think of anything else to do, other than mooning on Lori's doorstep, which he was pretty certain—especially now—she wouldn't have welcomed.

"Um, well, that's nice," Lori said, though the expression on her face added nothing to the banality.

Frustrated, Josh grabbed up a pencil. "Is there something wrong?"

She blinked. "Not at all."

The pencil snapped in two. "I'm going out to check on the progress at the Hip Hop site." He surged to his feet.

"All right."

Though the words were innocuous, for the first

time that day Josh detected a flicker of feeling on Lori's face. And the feeling, damn it all, was relief. As he came around his desk, she instantly turned and moved off to put distance between them.

"Lori," he said softly.

Her back to him, she halted. "What?"

"You're running away from me."

"I'm not." But she said it too quickly.

Josh inhaled a calming breath. "Okay. Fine. Whatever you say." Her shoulders appeared to relax, and the gesture ticked him off all over again. He made a quick calculation, then slid his hands into the pockets of his jeans. "I need you at the Hip Hop," he said.

She swung around. "Huh?"

He wasn't going to let her off so easily. "Yeah. I need you to…to take some notes."

Her eyebrows slammed together. "You what?"

"I need you to take some notes." He said it reasonably, as if he didn't have pencils and paper. As if he couldn't take his own notes, thank you very much.

Her mouth opened, then she closed it, apparently deciding against arguing with him. "I'll get my purse."

He smiled. "Perfect." If it took him the rest of the day in her company, he was going to figure out what was going on inside her beautiful, stubborn head.

He didn't have much luck on the car ride to the Hip Hop. Though he threw out a few generic comments, she let them slide past her with little more than a ladylike grunt or two.

She saved her animation, her smiles for Wyatt

North. When they ran in to the other man as they stepped into the newly framed building, Lori didn't hesitate to press him for the latest on Melissa's condition. Josh was interested himself. He still couldn't believe what Lori had told him about Melissa—that she'd been poisoned.

At the same moment, new husband and Whitehorn detective Mark Kincaid strode up. "Just who I've been looking for," he said to Wyatt. "I dropped by the hospital, but Melissa told me I'd find you here."

"So it's really true?" Josh asked Wyatt, looking over at Mark for confirmation too. "Someone intentionally tried to harm Melissa?"

"It's true." The determined expression on Mark's face made Josh remember that the other man had spent eight years on the New York City police force before returning to Whitehorn. "And I wish to God I could guarantee I'll find out who is behind the poisoning *and* the fire before Darcy and I leave on our honeymoon."

Wyatt didn't look any less determined. "Whether you find out who's behind it right away or not, *I* can guarantee nothing else—no one else—is going to hurt Melissa."

Josh shook his head. "I still don't understand. Poisoned? I just can't wrap my mind around that."

"It sounds crazy, doesn't it?" Mark answered. "But Noah Martin ran the tests twice. And because the only person affected at the wedding was Melissa, well, it comes way too soon after the arson for my peace of mind. I think someone has it in for her."

Lori, her face pale, made an anxious noise. Josh grabbed her hand. When she tried to pull away, he ignored her, warming her cold fingers between his. Then, through the open spaces in the wall studs, he caught sight of an odd couple picking their way through the Hip Hop parking lot.

He nodded in their direction, indicating Homer Gilmore and Connie Adams. Homer, a parka over his striped pajamas and ratty bathrobe, appeared to be mumbling to himself. In a wool coat and electric-blue beret, Connie Adams was close to his side. "Didn't someone mention Homer was complaining about the Hip Hop food?" Josh asked.

Wyatt and Mark exchanged a glance, and just then Connie looked up, catching sight of the group. Her face brightened and she linked her arm through Homer's to change his direction and tow him toward the framed entrance to the restaurant.

As she stepped over the threshold, she smiled brilliantly at Wyatt. "Just the man I wanted to see!" she called out gaily.

Wyatt's eyebrows rose, but Mark murmured to him quickly. "Distract her and give me a couple of minutes alone with Homer."

Wyatt sent Mark a pained look, but he moved obediently forward to meet Connie while the detective gave Homer a hearty hail and beckoned him closer. Stroking his long gray beard with nervous fingers, Homer inspected Mark out of the corner of his eyes and scuttled forward. "What do you want, Mr. Police?" Homer asked, his voice suspicious.

"Just wanted to know how you're doing, Homer," Mark said genially. "And what you've seen happening around town lately."

Homer stroked his hand over his beard again. He darted a look at Josh, then Lori. His hand slowed and his eyes narrowed. "Heard you were in the hospital," he said to her.

In Josh's hand, Lori's fingers jerked. "Me?"

"Lori?" Josh said, his gut knotting at the thought.

"Not Lori," Homer said. "Melissa. The one who makes that gawl-dang-awful stuff she calls hash."

"This is Lori," Mark said. "Not Melissa. But speaking of Melissa, Homer—"

"She looks like her," the old man grumbled, darting another glance at Lori. "Maybe somebody wanted to put *her* in the hospital and made a mistake," he went on. "Poison, arson," he mumbled under his breath.

A trickle, like icy water, ran down Josh's spine. "For God's sake, Homer—"

"You stop bothering him!" Connie's strident voice called out, and she broke away from her conversation with Wyatt to hurry over to her charge. "He's an old man. He doesn't know anything about anything." She glared at Josh, then Mark. "Let's go, Homer."

Within seconds, she'd whisked herself and the shuffling old man out of the restaurant. They headed across the street, Homer looking over his shoulder as if he was afraid of being followed.

Staring after them, Mark sighed. "I can't figure out if he's just an old coot or a crafty old coot."

Wyatt strolled up, shaking his head. "I can tell you that Connie is one for the record books anyway."

Josh looked over at his friend. "Why's that?"

"She just asked me out to dinner. My wife is in the hospital, the victim of poisoning, and I think that woman just propositioned me. Or was planning to, if I'd accepted her invitation."

The notion that Wyatt would consider for even one second Connie over his beloved wife Melissa made Josh smile. He looked down to share his amusement with Lori. Who didn't look amused at all. Instead, she appeared even more withdrawn, and the only color in her face was her sapphire eyes.

As the other two men launched into a discussion of possible motives for the arson and poisoning, Josh drew Lori away. "Are you all right?" He thought of crazy old Homer and what he'd said. "I hope you're not worried someone was really trying to poison you." He lowered his voice. "It's not your ex-husband, is it? You haven't seen or heard from him, have you?"

Lori shook her head. "No, I..." She swallowed. "But..." With a quick movement she slid her hand from Josh's grasp and turned away from him. "It's just that I don't know what he's capable of," she said, her voice a harsh whisper.

Josh stared at her stiff shoulders, her bent head, the tension evident in her spine. "What's the matter, Lori?"

"The dark side always turns up," she whispered. "There was the wedding and then the poisoning. I think I'm free of him, and then…what if this time he decides to hurt someone other than me?''

He froze. ''My God,'' he said. ''You…you…'' He couldn't finish the thought in words, but it sounded in his head all the same. She thought her ex-husband might come to Whitehorn and hurt someone. Not Lori, this time. But someone else. No wonder she was trying to distance herself again. It was just another way to protect herself.

''Oh, honey.'' His chest ached and he lifted his hand, then dropped it to his side. They were back to square one, he realized.

Josh drove them back to the construction office, his mind clicking over possibilities. He wasn't going to let Lori shut him out again. No way. It might take all the patience he could muster, but he was going to woo her back into his arms.

Tonight. He was afraid if he let her go too long she might turn from him altogether. She might find it was easy to live without him, just when he was learning how much he didn't want to live without her.

Unsure exactly how to go about breaking through to her, he left Lori alone for the rest of the afternoon. He wanted to get her away from the office, preferably at his home, but it wasn't until he happened to glance at the calendar on his desk that he thought of a way to lure her there.

He didn't bring it up until five o'clock, when she stood in his doorway, her purse clutched in her hands.

"I'm going home now," she said, her gaze trained somewhere over his left shoulder.

"Big plans for the evening?" he asked, keeping his voice casual.

Her eyes darted toward his face, darted away. "Um, well, the usual."

"If you're not too busy, I was hoping you could do me a big favor."

She darted another look at him, as if trying to gauge exactly what kind of "favor" he had in mind. He worked at keeping his expression bland.

"Well, um. Okay, I guess," she said.

He smiled. "Great. Let's go." As she sputtered in protest, he swept her toward the front door, turning off lights as he moved.

"Josh—"

"I only want a few minutes of your time," he lied. "I need a woman's...touch."

Her eyes narrowed. "What is it *exactly* that you want from me?"

He opened the front door and gestured her through. "Two of my sisters have birthdays next week. I bought two sweaters and I need help deciding which sister gets which one." As quickly as he could, he locked the office door, then set off toward the parking lot as if it was a given that she was following.

He heard her sigh and was grateful to the early-evening darkness for hiding his smile. "It won't take long," he said. *For me to ease you over your resistance.*

Josh took it as a good sign that she only sighed

again. In just a few short minutes, he pulled into his garage and she pulled in after him, to brake her car in his driveway.

He hurried inside and had the front door open, the heat turned up and the lights on, just as she mounted his porch steps. "What can I get you to drink?" he asked, as she crossed over the threshold.

"I won't be here long enough for that," she told him firmly.

"Okay." He shrugged. "Follow me, then." Whistling softly, he led the way into his bedroom.

Instead of stepping inside, she hovered on the threshold. "Josh. I don't know..."

Pretending not to understand the source of her hesitation, he pulled open the door to his walk-in closet. "Yes, I realize you don't know my sisters. But you're another woman, so your opinion is bound to be better than mine."

A bag in each hand, he exited the closet and approached his king-size bed. Without looking at Lori, he pulled out the sweaters and spread them against the caramel-colored comforter. One was cherry-red and casually styled. The other was dressier, indigo, with embroidered black flowers around the neckline.

His mother had selected them for him before she and his father had taken off on their latest trip.

"What do you think?" Trying to appear completely innocent and somewhat baffled, he gestured toward them with his hand, then looked over at Lori.

His breath caught in his lungs. As he'd been fetching the sweaters, she'd been busy too. The top two buttons of her blouse were unfastened and she was combing her fingers through her newly released hair.

It wasn't a come-on, her little frown and focus on the sweaters made that clear, but she looked softer than she had all day. Warmer.

And she was four feet from his bed.

She stepped closer, and her hand left her hair to stroke the texture of each sweater. Josh thought of that hand stroking him and he closed his eyes.

"You have good taste, Josh," she said. "Both these sweaters are beautiful."

He opened his eyes, smiled, tried his best to look innocent again. "Thanks. But I still don't know which one to give Elaine and which one to give Lisa."

Lori tilted her head, her gaze on the sweaters. "Tell me about them." She sat down on the edge of the bed.

Josh considered pushing her back against the mattress. He thought about the five buttons of her blouse that were still fastened and how warm and peachy the skin beneath would taste.

"Josh?" A note of wariness entered her voice.

He cleared his throat. The point was to woo her, not worry her, he reminded himself. "Let's see. Elaine is my oldest sister. She's the tomboy of the three. The one that taught me how to throw a curveball, as a matter of fact. On the other hand, Lisa is the beauty queen of the family. We used to have to yell 'Fire!' to get her out of the bathroom."

"Hmm." Lori pressed her lips together and touched each sweater again, obviously considering.

"I think the more casual sweater for Elaine then, and the one with the flowers for Lisa." Against the creaminess of her skin, her lips stood out, rosy-pink.

His mind not on anything but her mouth, and the taste of it that he remembered so well, Josh shook his head. "Nah." His mother had told him that Elaine would love the blue, and Lisa the red. Lori's eyes rounded in surprise at his instant rejection of her advice, and he quickly caught himself. "I mean, do you really think so?"

"Josh…"

Hell, there was that wary note again. As if it was the most casual thing in the world, he dropped to the mattress too, sitting on the other side of the sweaters. With a frown, he pretended to look them over. "Maybe I should have bought them toasters or something."

"These are much better than toasters," Lori said. "I promise you. Why don't you tell me what they look like?"

Thinking quickly—Lord, he was such a smart guy—he bounced off the bed and jogged into the den for a photo album. He was back in his bedroom and back on the bed—*beside* Lori this time—before she had a chance to guess his ulterior motive.

His thigh pressed against hers as he opened the leather-covered book so that it crossed both their laps. The first page displayed a photograph of the Anderson family—three big sisters huddled around a blanket-wrapped bundle that was Josh.

She laughed. "Is this you?"

He savored the first light-hearted sound she'd made all day. "Three days old." With a finger he indicated first one little girl and then another. "That's Elaine. That's Lisa. The one who looks like she's about to pinch me is the sister closest to me in age, Dana."

Lori turned the next page herself, and laughed again as she took in the two-page spread of Josh in various stages of undress. "Not very modest, are we?"

He didn't try to suppress a grin. "Hey, even at two months old I knew—when you got it, you gotta flaunt it." With his elbow, he gave her a teasing jab. "Wouldn't you agree?"

Lori looked up from the album, amused. Josh stared at her beautiful face, so achingly close. His own humor evaporated, replaced by hunger as his gaze ran from her eyes to her mouth to the pulse beating, suddenly frantic, in her throat.

She hastily dropped her gaze and turned several more pages until the photos showed the girls as teenagers. "Well," Lori said, her head studiously bent over the album. "It looks to me as if Elaine's dark hair would be perfect with the red sweater and Lisa's blond with the blue."

That pulse was still drumming in a frenzied rhythm at the base of her throat. Josh shook his head, thinking only of what it would feel like, beating against his tongue. "Elaine's favorite color is blue. Lisa's devoted to red."

Lori paused. "You didn't want my opinion at all, did you Josh?"

He winced. "It's not that I didn't *want* your opinion..."

She looked up, pinned him with her eyes. "You didn't *need* it then."

"Lori, I—" He closed his mouth, opened it, ran his hands through his hair, only the truth in his mind. "I need you."

Her gaze shifted away, and she shoved the album off her legs in order to stand. "I should go."

"Why, damn it?" He hated the feeling she was slipping away from him. He pushed the album onto the mattress and stood too. Then with an effort, he softened his voice, remembering he had to charm her if he could. "I thought we agreed to give what we have some time. A chance."

Her fingers wove together in front of her. "I—" She broke off, shrugged.

Josh took a long breath, dredging up every scrap of patience he could find inside himself. He knew she'd been hurt. Frightened. He knew he had to tread lightly. "Just a chance, Lori."

But she shook her head and started for the doorway. "No, Josh," she said. "I don't think—"

"Don't think!" As if from a great distance, Josh saw himself bolt toward her, take her arm and spin her around. This wasn't wooing her, this wasn't charming her, this wasn't treading lightly. He knew it wasn't, but if doing those meant letting her get away, then to hell with patience.

His blood rushed through him in a blaze of heat. He shook his head, trying to clear his suddenly hazy vision, trying to shake his senses back into order, but there was only Lori. Her eyes, her mouth, the beauty that he couldn't let walk away from him without a fight.

His hand tightened on her arm. He hauled her close, yanked her to her toes. Bending his head, he kissed her. Hard.

Chapter Twelve

Lori's body stiffened beneath Josh's hands. He cursed himself and eased up on her mouth, but he couldn't, wouldn't let her go. "Honey," he murmured. "Lori."

She turned her face, so his lips ran across her cheek. "Josh," she said, the ache in her voice echoing the ache in his heart. "I'm worried that—"

"No." He wasn't going to let her worry. That was worse than thinking. "Just kiss me," he demanded.

She still hesitated, then slowly, so slowly, she turned her face back to his.

And that was the last time he asked her for anything that night.

With her mouth beneath his once more, Josh lost all finesse, all patience. Desire burned in his blood and he couldn't think of anything but bringing her against him, with him. His hands slid to the open V of her blouse, his fingers curling over the edges of the material as he kissed her. When her tongue met his, his hands jerked.

Buttons pinged as they scattered across the hardwood floor, but the sound barely registered over the heavy thump of his heart. The skin of her shoulders was warm under his palms, and he followed her racing goose bumps as he pushed the sleeves of her blouse off her arms.

The still-fastened cuffs trapped the blouse at her wrists, but he was too needy to fool with it any longer. Instead, he left it hanging, concentrating on all the creamy skin between her mouth and her bra. He licked it, sucked on it, drew its scent into his lungs.

Then he buried his face in the valley of her breasts, her heartbeat against his lips, her softness against his cheeks. He felt her shudder, but he also heard her moan, so he didn't stop.

He couldn't stop.

His mouth settled over her lace-covered nipple. He sucked it in, closing his eyes as it hardened against his tongue. His hands ran down her back, over her hips, cupping her buttocks to press her body against his erection.

He surged against her, his body seeking. Desperate for more of her, he lifted his shaking fingers and unlatched the front clasp of her bra. The cups parted and he pushed the bra straps toward her wrists, too.

She cried out when he fastened his mouth on her

bare nipple. The sound made him pause, but then she arched her back, offering more of herself to him.

His head spun. Need driving him like a whip, he lifted her into his arms. Somehow he found her nipple again, latched onto it and felt her jerk. But she wasn't shrinking away from him, she was lifting herself still closer, and he gave her what she silently asked for.

Sucking strongly, he turned toward the bed. He opened his eyes to find his way, and the sight of her half-bared body bowing in his arms caused another deluge of lust to rush through his blood. Groaning, he reached back to flip off the light, hoping the darkness would slow down his heated response.

But it only made the night more intimate.

He had to feel her, skin-to-skin.

The photo album thumped to the floor as he pushed it aside to lay Lori against the bed linens. His fingers fumbling in haste, he worked on his own shirt, only managing to undo a couple of buttons before he grabbed the tails and pulled the thing over his head.

His jeans came next, and he threw them off with the same amount of impatience. He rolled on a condom, then his fingers found the button of her pants. He tore at it, frustrated when the tab of the zipper stuck. Finally it gave, and he slid the fabric down over her long, silky thighs.

She wore boots, and he gritted his teeth in frustration as he worked them off. Then, finally then, she was naked.

He climbed onto the mattress, then moved between her legs, the sleek skin of her inner thighs gliding against his knees as he sought the place where he wanted to bury himself.

The head of his shaft just touching her slick heat, he froze, his body shuddering at the sensation. He sat back on his heels. "It's so damn good." His voice was guttural, hard.

His palms ran up the inside of her thighs, then he pushed his thumbs through the springy hair at their apex. His body still against hers, connected only by the most delicate of sexual kisses, he pushed her folds open and found the nub hidden there.

He stroked it, the callused tips of his thumbs strumming it one after the other. Lori moaned, but he didn't stop. Couldn't stop making her respond.

"I do this to you," he said. The coiling tension in her body was obvious as she lifted her hips, causing her body to swallow two inches of his. He groaned, fighting the lure of that hot, tight glove, as his fingers continued to provoke her, tease her. "You're mine."

Her hips tilted higher, trying to take more of him. Closing his eyes, he lifted himself away, not giving her another inch. His fingers continued playing; her body strained.

"Josh…" She was pleading for him, for release. But he was in control here. Every response was his to command, the fire inside her his to stoke. Tonight, every sensation in her body was his.

He took her high, reading the level of her passion in the trembling muscles in her body and in her ragged breath. With her hands still trapped by her blouse, she couldn't touch him, and he liked that too, he liked that she was completely at his mercy.

Then, when she finally let out a passionate sob, he relented. He firmed his touch, stroking her faster, harder. She sucked in one shallow breath, her body bowed one final time, then it shook, jerking against his in unmistakable pleasure.

While the waves were still moving through her, Josh let himself go. And plunged.

Her body convulsed around his, milking pleasure from his invasion. Josh gritted his teeth, trying to prolong the sweet agony, but Lori defeated him. Her inner muscles closed around him on another pulse of passion and he plunged deep, drew out, plunged deeper.

His release surged out of his heart. Like a shout of desperation it came from the deep depths of his soul. Fierce delight flashed through him, shook him, and he poured it into Lori's body, trying to give back everything he'd taken.

He came back to himself moments—hours?—later. His skin went cold as he realized he was on top of her. *He was holding her down.*

"Lori. I…" He rolled off her, landing on the other pillow. He threw his arm over his face. "I'm sorry…I wasn't thinking."

My God, he was supposed to be wooing her! Instead, desperate not to lose her, he'd manhandled her, forcing her to respond to him, forcing her to take his touch on *his* terms. His gut clenched. "I'm so damn sorry."

In the darkness, he couldn't see her face, he didn't sense her movement. Somehow she'd freed herself from her blouse and now her palm cupped his cheek. He flinched, the gentle touch stinging more than a slap. "Josh," she said. He couldn't read the tone of her voice. "You have to know I liked it."

He hauled in a deep breath. "I know you…that I satisfied you. But Lori, I know I was all over you. I know I didn't give you much, if any, choice."

"Josh, it's okay—"

"It's *not* okay. I wanted you to know that you could trust me. I betrayed that."

"Oh, Josh." Somehow, she found his hand and brought it to her cheek. Her face was wet.

Oh, no. She'd been crying.

"Lori—"

"Just shut up, Josh," she said, though there was no anger in her voice.

"But you're crying."

"Because I'm happy." She pressed his hand harder against her soft skin. "I *do* trust you, Josh. Do you think I could have enjoyed myself so much if I didn't? For the last four years I've wondered if I'd ever be normal again. Have normal responses. Not be afraid. Tonight, with you, Josh, I felt normal. I wasn't afraid. Not for one instant."

Something twisted in his chest. "Honey, I…" At a loss for words, he reached for her, closing his arms gently around her body.

"I won't break," she said, sighing as she snuggled closer.

But he might. He was weak with gratitude. He closed his eyes and rubbed his cheek against the top of her head. "Lori," he said. "We've got to give this a chance."

He could have told her his heart, his love, required it, but there was only so much a man could demand in one night. Her mouth touched the center of his bare chest. "I know," she whispered.

Josh drifted off to sleep. When he woke some time later, he blinked, dazzled for a moment by the glow of the bedside lamp. Lori was sitting up on the pillows beside him, the sheet tucked under her arms and the photograph album open in her lap.

He watched her in silence for a moment, enjoying the sight of her in his bed almost as much as the little smile playing over her mouth as she turned the pages. Then she stilled, her expression turning serious.

Curious at the sudden change in her mood, Josh lifted onto his elbow to peer at the page. Then their gazes met.

"She made a beautiful bride," Lori said.

Josh glanced down at the wedding photograph of his wife Kay, then looked back at Lori. He half smiled. "Yes. She did."

Lori lifted her hand, then let it drift back to the mattress. "It...hurts me, to think of you having to go through that grief," she said. She shook her head as if the emotion puzzled her. "I know this is going to sound weird, but I wish I could have been with you. I wish I could have been here to help you through it."

Josh's heart twisted. In what other ways was Lori going to slay him? "I wasn't alone. I had my family with me. My parents, sisters, all the cousins and aunts and uncles. The worst part was…"

Lori reached out and brushed his hair off his forehead. "Was what? I want to know."

"The worst part was that I knew I had taken our time together for granted. There were things I didn't know about Kay. Depths I'd thought I had all our lives to explore." Or maybe he hadn't cared enough to explore them. Sometimes that thought tortured him, too. "Maybe I didn't love her enough."

Lori shook her head. "You loved her as a man of your age and experience loves." With one finger she touched the photo, tracing Josh and Kay's figures.

"I didn't understand her." The words slipped out.

Lori's gaze met his. "Do you think we ever completely know someone's heart? Do you think it's possible?"

He sat up, the sheet pooling around his waist. "I think we have to be willing to show our hearts to those we love. Maybe not from the very first. Maybe not all at once." His gaze dropped to Kay's photo, her face smiling, her mind still a mystery. "But maybe…maybe she thought she couldn't trust me."

"No." Lori reached out and touched his forearm, her fingers circling firmly. "Take it from me, Josh."

"I wanted a partner," Josh said, covering her hand with his free one. "Someone to share with me dreams and fears." Then he groaned, realizing what he was saying. "How romantic is this? I want you to give *us* a chance and all I'm doing is talking about someone else.''

Lori smiled. There was something in her eyes, a light, an understanding, that made her even more beautiful. ''But your past is part of you, Josh. And I want to know all the parts. Every one.''

He shut the photo album and dropped it over the side of the bed in order to gather Lori against his chest. The sheet covering hers dropped and his interest caught on what was newly revealed.

Her nipples hardened as he watched.

Bending his head, he kissed her cheek, her mouth, her ear. ''I have a part of me that wants to get to know you better right this very minute.''

She shivered, but there was amusement in her voice. ''You're bad, do you know that?''

He reached over to turn out the light. ''That's the part I'm talking about.''

A few mornings later, Lori parked outside the Big Sky Five & Dime, across the street from the Hip Hop construction site. Since the day before, warm, dry chinook winds had been flowing off the eastern Rocky Mountains. Josh said the Native Americans called these winds ''snow eaters,'' and Lori could see why. Melted snow ran in shallow rivers down the White-horn streets and her sneakers landed in a puddle of it as she stepped out of her car.

But the almost seventy-degree weather was glorious! She nearly laughed out loud at the glorious sensation of warmth brushing against her bare arms below her short-sleeved shirt. It was as if Montana's weather was reflecting Lori's own springlike mood.

On a day like today, Lori thought as she pushed open the door of the Big Sky Five & Dime, anything was possible.

To cap off an already stellar morning, the first person Lori saw as she entered the store was her half sister Melissa, browsing through a rack of greeting cards. There was color in the other woman's cheeks and a smile curved her lips as she caught sight of Lori.

"Hello there," she said. "Is it just the weather or am I right in thinking that you look extremely happy?"

Lori didn't try to hold back her smile. "All's right with my world," she replied. "And you—you look happy *and* well. No repercussions from your illness?" Though she'd spoken with Melissa on the phone twice since her release from the hospital, this was the first time she'd talked with her face-to-face.

"Unless you call Wyatt's overprotectiveness a repercussion, then no." Melissa leaned toward Lori. "We met Josh at the Hip Hop earlier and I snuck away from the guy talk. This is the first time Wyatt's left me alone since I went into the hospital."

Lori remembered the strain on Wyatt's face when he was keeping his vigil at Melissa's bedside. "He doesn't want anything else to happen to you."

Melissa grimaced. "Believe me, I don't want another repeat either. But I need a little room to breathe, you know? Speaking of sharing space..." She wiggled her eyebrows in mischievous suggestion. "Josh let drop that you two are, um, keeping company."

Even though Melissa was her half sister, Lori wasn't quite ready to share the delirious state of her heart. "That's who I'm here to see," she said, side-stepping the issue. "I thought I'd bring some coffee over for him and the crew."

"Hey, good idea. I'll get some for Wyatt too, then maybe he'll forgive me for running off on him."

It only took a few minutes for the two of them to go to the Five & Dime's counter and get a couple of cardboard carriers filled with paper cups of coffee. Then, chatting away, they walked across the street toward the Hip Hop's doorless entry. The roof and exterior siding had been completed and now the men were working inside.

Still talking, Lori followed Melissa through the doorway, then her train of thought derailed, leaving her mouth hanging open with nothing coherent coming out.

Outdoors was warm, but it was even warmer inside the Hip Hop. So warm, in fact, that several of the construction crew had stripped off their shirts. But Lori couldn't look away from one man's naked torso. From Josh.

Standing on a ladder a few feet away, a tool belt slung around his slim, jeans-encased hips, Josh was hammering on a sheet of drywall. With each stroke, the heavy muscles of his back bunched then shifted, the fluid movements an undeniable testament to male strength.

A few weeks ago, such a demonstration of masculine power would have made her queasy.

Melissa laughed softly. "You're drooling from the corner of your mouth."

Lori swallowed. "I—I don't think so. I don't think I can be drooling and terrified all at the same time." Her stomach was clenching, twisting in a vain attempt to get away from the truth.

"Terrified?" Melissa said, her voice full of concern. "Lori, what's the matter?"

Lori inhaled a long breath, hoping a large dose of oxygen would cure her. "I'm, well, terrified that I'm *not* terrified." Shaking her head, she even managed a small laugh. "As crazy as that sounds."

"It sounds interesting," Melissa replied. "I reserve judgment on crazy until I hear more."

Josh's arm swung again, an energy-filled arc. The sunlight streaming through one window opening caught a bead of sweat rolling down the shallow valley of his spine. He grunted as the head of his hammer hit the nail. Lori's stomach clenched again.

"I—" Lori started, stopped, trying to gather her composure. "Men—their brawn, their force—used to make me nervous. Wary."

"And now?"

"Josh, he's made me understand—believe—that a man can be tough, but tender too. I...I think I'm in love with him." Lori looked at Melissa, not sure what the other woman would think.

Melissa's expression was serious. "Did you just figure this out?"

"I— Yes." Lori looked back at Josh. "When I walked in here, when I saw him, his body, his strength, I thought he was beautiful, not something to be wary of." She shrugged, helpless to explain it any further.

"I'm thrilled for you," Melissa said. "Josh and you are both lucky."

Lucky wasn't exactly how Lori felt. She stared at her half sister. "But what if…"

"I know he feels the same," Melissa said. "Don't worry about that." She nodded in Josh's direction. "Look at the expression on the man's face. Why do you think he's smiling?"

His head turned toward the women, Josh was descending the ladder. A few rungs from the bottom, he leaped down, sliding his hammer into a loop of his tool belt as he approached them. Melissa was right, he was smiling.

Lori swallowed, but found she was unable to speak again. She mutely held out the carrier of coffees.

Josh didn't need words, apparently, to know when something important was going through her mind. His eyes narrowed. "What's wrong, honey?"

"Nothing's wrong," Melissa answered for her.

His gaze still on Lori, one of Josh's eyebrows rose.

Lori swallowed again. "I'm fine," she said, her voice a half-croak. "I brought the crew coffee."

"You're an angel." Josh smiled, then shouted for the crew to come over. As several men approached, including Wyatt, Josh bent near and kissed Lori's cheek. "The kind of angel a man could get used to waking up to," he whispered against her ear.

Lori's face heated, but she was saved from having to respond by the arrival of the men. The coffees were passed around and the group stood together, gulping down the hot stuff and talking about the construction's progress.

Josh had tucked his T-shirt in the back pocket of his jeans and now he pulled it free and slipped it on. Lori smiled, wondering what he would think about his "angel" if she told him how disappointed she was to lose sight of all that naked skin of his.

Catching her smile, he slanted her an inquiring look. She shook her head, biting back her grin. With a shrug, he grabbed up the last coffee then casually slung his free arm around her. With a little sigh, Lori leaned back against him. His fingers tightened briefly—sweetly—on her side.

After a few minutes of conversation, the construction crew began drifting back to their places. The last man started to leave, but then he turned back, snapping his fingers.

"Hey, seeing you two ladies together reminds me." The young man, Scott, gestured toward Lori and Melissa, who were standing side-by-side, sandwiched by Josh and Wyatt. "There was a guy asking after you this morning."

"Oh?" Melissa slipped Wyatt's coffee cup from his hand and took a sip from it. "Was it that restaurant supplier from Big Timber? He doesn't seem to believe me when I tell him I'll call him as soon as I'm ready to make my order.''

"Nah.'' Scott shook his head. "He wasn't asking after you.''

Melissa laughed. "I thought you just said he was.''
Scott shook his head. "I meant he was asking about Lori.''

Josh's fingers twitched, just as Lori felt a cold chill rush over her skin. "Me?'' she said, her voice croaking again.

"Yeah. He said he was an old friend of yours. That he wanted to surprise you.'' Scott grimaced. "Whoops. Hope I didn't just ruin it.''

Lori's heartbeat jumped to panic-rhythm. *Oh God,* she thought. *What am I going to do now?*

Before she could form a coherent thought, Josh spoke up. "Scott,'' he said. "What did this man look like and what exactly did you say to him?''

At the clipped tone of his boss's voice, Scott gave a nervous roll of his shoulders. "I hope I didn't—''

"What he looked like, what you said,'' Josh interjected.

Scott rolled his shoulders again. "I'm not sure how old he is. Thirty-five, maybe? Thin, blond. He asked if I knew Lori. He asked if I knew where she lived or worked.''

It was definitely David, Lori thought, a high whine starting in her ears. "What did you tell him?'' she asked Scott.

Scott darted a look at Josh, then back at her. "I didn't think Josh would want some guy looking you up at work. I don't know where you live. But I did tell him that you spend a lot of time at the gym at the high school.'' His face reddened. ''I've, um, noticed you running when I lift weights.''

''Okay,'' Lori said. Though it wasn't okay. Nothing was going to be okay again.

''What's the matter?'' Wyatt asked. ''Do you know this man, Lori?''

''He's my ex-husband.'' Lori bit her bottom lip. ''I, um, wasn't expecting to see him again.''

''How do you think he found you?'' Josh said, his face a stiff, unreadable mask.

Lori shook her head. ''I'm not sure. I know I never told him about Whitehorn. But maybe my mother did.''

Josh's eyebrows rose. ''Your mother knew Whitehorn?''

Lori blinked, realizing she'd never told Josh about her mother growing up in the town. Just as she'd never told Melissa they were half sisters. ''I—''

''Come to think of it, he did mention something about you too, Mrs. North,'' Scott suddenly said.

The hairs on the back of Lori's neck lifted and the whine in her ears jumped an octave higher. ''What exactly did he say?'' she asked, trying to keep her voice calm.

Apparently she didn't do too good a job, because Wyatt cursed. Scott looked as if he wanted the particle board beneath his feet to open up and swallow him. ''Just that he'd seen an article in the newspaper about Mrs. North's being in the hospital. That her photograph looked a lot like the woman he was trying to locate. That's why he stopped by the Hip Hop to ask about Lori.''

Oh God, oh God, oh God. Lori took a step back, her gaze swinging toward Melissa and Wyatt. ''You need to be careful,'' she said.

Josh grabbed her arm. ''Lori—''

''No.'' She shook him off. ''Listen to me,'' she said to Melissa. ''David, my ex-husband, he's a dangerous man. And we do resemble each other. Be sure you let Wyatt take care of you.''

''Lori.'' Melissa's expression was puzzled. ''So we look alike. Several people have mentioned it to me already. But what does that have to do with—''

''It just does,'' Lori said, knowing she sounded crazy and not caring, not as long as Melissa and Wyatt heeded her warning. If David had made a connection between her and Melissa, if he knew—or guessed—they were family, then her sister could be in danger. She wouldn't put it past David to harm someone Lori cared about in order to hurt her.

''Lori, what's going on?'' Josh asked the question on all their faces.

''I...I have something I have to do,'' Lori said. ''You'll have to excuse me.'' She had to get out of Whitehorn. Leave right away before David discovered her or discovered for certain that Melissa was her sister.

Or discovered that Josh was the man Lori loved.

No one, especially not Josh who was as straightforward as he was strong, was a match for the kind of deviousness David was capable of. "I'll see you back at the office," she lied to Josh. When he returned there, he would find a note, not Lori.

"You're not going anywhere without me," he said through his teeth.

She shook her head. "Back at the office." Then she turned and ran.

Chapter Thirteen

Melting snow shushed beneath Josh's tires as he sped back to the office. His fingers squeezed the steering wheel during the short drive, only easing when he spied Lori's car in the construction office's parking lot.

He pulled in beside it, braked, then jumped out. His heart pounding against his chest, he ran toward the front entrance. Just as he reached it, the door swung open and Lori stepped out, her arms around a cardboard box full of her belongings.

Josh's stomach cramped. "What the hell do you think you're doing?"

Lori stared at him. "I—I told you I'd see you here later."

He put his hands on her shoulders and pushed her

back inside, then slammed the door shut behind them. "Thank God I didn't believe you. Because you wouldn't have been here, would you?"

A guilty flush reddened her cheeks. "Well, I…"

Josh set his back teeth and gave a pointed look at the things inside the box she was carrying. Her purse, her coffee mug, her briefcase, the potted African violet he'd surprised her with last week. "Damn it, Lori," he said, more frustrated than he could ever remember. "What the hell are you thinking?"

She looked down at the violets. "I'm thinking this isn't working out very well. I need…I need a new job."

"What?"

"I said I—"

"I know what you said." Josh grabbed the box from her and set it on the floor. Then he grasped her wrist and tugged her toward the reception area. "Sit." He pointed toward one of the chairs.

Darting a nervous look outside the office windows, she perched on the seat. Even though it was near seventy degrees outside, the temperature in the office seemed icy to him. To give him time to get hold of his temper, Josh stoked the small fire in the wood-burning stove. When it was kicking out some decent heat, he pulled a chair closer to Lori's and sat down at right angles to her, their knees almost touching.

"Now," he said. "We're going to solve this thing with your ex-husband."

Lori blew out an impatient breath of air, riffling her

dark bangs in the process. "We can't 'solve' it, Josh. I tried, the police tried, the courts tried."

He waved off all that. "First, you're going to move in with me."

She shook her head. "No."

He held onto his temper. "Why not?"

"It won't solve anything."

"Of course it will," he snapped back. "It will keep you safe."

An expression crossed her face, sadness maybe, or defeat. "This is about more than just me."

Josh's eyes narrowed. "Yes. What's all this about Melissa?" He paused, thinking back to the conversation in the Hip Hop. "And Whitehorn. What was this you mentioned about your mother and Whitehorn?"

Lori lifted her hand, let it fall. "I guess I never told you that my mother used to live in Whitehorn."

Josh took a breath. "I guess you never did," he said slowly, his voice filled with irony.

"She grew up here. Then...then she moved to the South where I was born. When I was looking for someplace else to live, I thought of here because..." Lori shrugged.

"But you said David didn't know about Whitehorn?"

"I didn't think so." She shrugged again. "The last few months of my mother's life she spoke about a lot of things she had never told me before. Her childhood, her past. Personal things."

"Whitehorn was one of them?"

Lori nodded. "Before that, she'd always been very hush-hush about her life before South Carolina. It's why I never thought she'd have told David." Her gaze shifted toward the windows again. "I guess I was wrong."

Josh didn't even bother looking outside. Just let Lori's ex-husband come near her. He'd welcome the bastard to Montana in his very own personal way. "What exactly does any of this have to do with Melissa?"

Lori's gaze jumped to his. "N-nothing."

He shook his head. "Won't wash, honey."

She hesitated, then her shoulders slumped. "I suppose it doesn't matter. Not now," she muttered to herself.

"What doesn't matter?"

"I…" Lori closed her eyes, opened them. "I came to Whitehorn because I wanted to be where my mother grew up. And I wanted to get to know my half sister."

Josh stilled. "Melissa?" His mind whirled. The resemblance, Lori's interest in the other woman, it all made sense. "Why didn't you ever say anything?"

"I wasn't sure what to say. Or do. What if she didn't like me? What if she didn't like me because I was the product of an affair between her father and my mother? I wanted to give us a chance to know each other first, without bringing the past into it."

Josh listened to her oh-so-reasonable explanation, his mood growing darker by the minute. "Hell, Lori, I meant why didn't you ever tell *me?*"

She blinked. "I—" Her mouth clamped shut.

"You never even considered it, did you?" His voice was harsh. While he'd been opening himself to her, while he'd been wooing her, *loving* her, she'd been clutching her secrets to herself as tightly as ever.

Her expression closed. Then she stood up. "I have to go."

Josh grabbed her wrist. "When you go, we'll go together. Let me gather a few things and then I'll follow you over to my house. We can work at home today."

"No," Lori said.

Josh sighed. "We don't need to stop by your place, Lori. Not now, anyway. We'll get your things later."

"No." Lori shook her head. "I'm not moving in with you."

Josh reined in his sudden spike of anger. "Don't be stupid. You'll be safer at my house."

"I'm leaving Whitehorn. Today. Right now."

He just stared at her, her words echoing in his head. "You're leaving me?"

Her mouth set. She nodded. "It's for the best."

"Lori—"

"I'll be fine."

The three words turned back the clock five years and his temper exploded. "*Fine?* What the hell kind of word is that?"

Lori swallowed. "I'll be fine on my own."

"Meaning you don't need me," he said flatly. "You don't need my protection."

She swallowed again. "Yes."

"You don't need my help."

"Yes."

Josh stared at her. "You're just like Kay," he said. Lori flinched. "I don't know what you mean."

"Rash. Foolhardy. Unable to ask for help when you need it."

"I told you," Lori answered, her voice fierce. "I'm not weak. I don't need help."

Josh's anger spiked again as he realized how serious Lori was. Her face was set and her eyes were hard. His heart twisted and he grimaced. This was pain he'd never wanted to feel again.

"Damn it. Damn it." He jumped to his feet and paced around the reception area. "What the hell is wrong with me?"

Lori rose to her feet, too. "Josh, it's not—" She broke off, started again. "Believe me, there's nothing wrong with you."

As if that little assurance was going to take the edge off. "Yeah?" He shook his head. "Then how do you explain me finding, me *loving*, the one woman in the world who wants to put me through this kind of hell again?"

Lori's face paled. "You…love me?"

"No. I couldn't possibly." He stalked to the window and braced his hands on the sill. "I won't do this again. I blamed myself for Kay's death, and the truth is, I blamed her too. How could she be so foolish? If she'd thought of me, been willing to share more of herself with me, she wouldn't have taken such a pointless risk that day."

"I don't know what drove Kay. But I know I can't lean on you, Josh. I can't let myself be weak in that way." Lori's voice sounded strained. "I'm leaving town right now. I'll be safe that way. I'm not doing it to hurt you, Josh."

Then why was his chest aching? He closed his eyes. Steeled himself. "And you're not going to hurt me." He turned his head and looked at her, willing it to be true. "I told you, I don't just want a lover. I want a partner, a life partner. Well, you've just proven that you can't be that."

"Josh—"

"Go ahead and leave town, Lori." The words tasted like ashes in his mouth, but he had to find a way to survive without her. "Leave Whitehorn with a clear conscience. Because I don't love you. I *won't* love you."

"I know." Lori's voice cracked.

So did Josh's heart. He whirled around.

She was speeding toward the door and had wrenched it open before he could stop her. Her hair fluttered behind her as she ran out.

"Lori!" He rushed to the open doorway, only to come face-to-face with someone new.

"Hey, Mr. Anderson." A kid marched up, in the uniform white shirt and dark pants of the nearby parochial school. He held out a glossy brochure. "We have the day off and I'm selling herbs and stuff for a school fundraiser." The kid paused, then grinned. "How many can I sign you up for?"

The interruption made Josh pause for a crucial moment. Just as he was digging for some cash to shove at the kid, he saw Lori's car tear out of the parking lot.

Though her eyes were dry, Lori's breath came in hiccupy sobs as she drove the short distance to her apartment. She'd made it out of the construction office without betraying the shattered state of her heart, but once inside her car she hadn't been able to control her feelings.

Still, she had to believe that leaving town was the right choice to make.

It was one thing to forge a relationship with Josh and with Melissa when David was a threat she'd left behind. It was entirely another to bring that threat into the lives of these two people she cared so much about.

People that she loved.

As she braked in her apartment's parking lot, she blinked back the tears stinging her eyes. *Josh loved her.* No, that wasn't right. If he *had* loved her, he didn't anymore.

Pulling her keys from her purse, she rushed up the path to her front door. Getting out of Whitehorn was the thing to think about now. Not Josh.

Once inside, she double-locked her door and dragged her suitcases from the narrow hall closet. There were only her clothes and a few personal items to pack. After years of looking over her shoulder she'd learned the importance of being able to pick up and move on quickly. Like the last three places she'd lived, she'd rented the apartment furnished.

Once she'd stuffed everything into her luggage, she took one last look around. Her gaze snagged on a flannel shirt of Josh's, one he'd left behind after spending the night in her bed.

She stared at it, biting down on her lower lip. She *had* to leave him, for God's sake. What kind of woman could profess to love a man in one breath, then put him in danger in another?

Josh thought he could handle David. But so had she, and she had the scars to prove how wrong she'd been. She swallowed hard, trying to rein in another rush of regret. This wasn't the time or place to second-guess herself! She knew David was in White-horn. And deep in her soul, call it instinct, call it intuition, she sensed that he was more determined than ever. He'd come all the way to Montana, hadn't he?

She could almost smell the evil stench of the de-mons that drove her ex-husband. She could almost hear their vicious whispers.

Lori rushed back into the bedroom and slammed shut one of her suitcases then grabbed for the handle. It slipped from her grasp, thumping to the carpet, and Lori stared down at her nerveless fingers. They quaked, her hands trembling like an old woman's.

She wouldn't be able to drive like this. Lord, she'd kill herself or someone else before she made it two blocks.

Her breath hiccuped again, and she closed her eyes, willing herself to calm. But instead, faces kaleidoscoped in her imagination: Josh, Melissa—David. Their images shattered, reformed, shattered again.

She dropped onto the mattress. If only she could find the kind of peace she found when running. The kind of tranquility she found in the zone.

Her gaze landed on the one still-open suitcase, her running shoes tucked into one corner. If only she could put them on and run away from her problems!

She looked down at her shaking hands. Why not? Of course she couldn't run away from her problems, but why couldn't she go for a calming run before leaving town?

Because David had been told about her habit of visiting the gym, that's why. If he operated as he had all the other times he'd found her, right now he was parked in the gym parking lot, patiently waiting for her to show up.

But a new thought jumped into her mind. It was nearly seventy degrees outside. Why couldn't she take her run outside? With David staked out at the gym, she could take one last goodbye run around White-horn before driving away from the town forever.

Without letting herself think on it anymore, Lori started dressing in her running clothes. It took her a long time; her fingers were still almost useless, but her panic was easing.

She knew she was taking a chance. But she needed this. She needed to run the Whitehorn streets one time and pretend that it was her town. Pretend that her life was her own.

Her fingers fumbled again as she locked her apartment door, but then she slipped the key into the interior pocket of her shorts. Nerves strung tight, she didn't go through her usual stretching. Instead, she started out jogging, letting the slow, deliberate steps warm up her muscles.

The Montana air was sweet and she sucked it in, trying to capture this precursor of a Whitehorn spring that she wouldn't be here to see. She passed the occasional person as she headed out, but for the most part, the streets she moved along were quiet and semirural.

As her pace sped up she anticipated that blissful zone. Surely by the next corner she'd be there. Or the next.

But it didn't happen. Her mind didn't smooth out as she so desperately needed it to do. Instead, it filled with Josh. With his slow smile, his slow lovemaking, the desperate and angry edge to his voice after she'd told him she was leaving.

She wasn't wrong to leave him!

Was she?

Once that little doubt entered her mind, she couldn't seem to shake it. Her feet moved faster, trying to outrun it, but instead it kept pace with her. With every step the question jabbed at her.

By staying, by counting on Josh, by *leaning* on him, then he would have power over her. That was a kind of vulnerability she'd sworn never to feel again the day she'd crossed the state line into Montana. Relying on herself, training and honing her own strength so that she could do that, was what had kept her sane all these years David had been stalking her.

Josh wanted a partner, and she couldn't be that.

Her footsteps faltered. *A partner.*

Josh wanted to share with a woman. He wanted a woman's dreams, her emotions, her strength. In return he wanted to give his own back. Give and take. Take and give.

She thought of the anguished expression on his face when she'd said she was going away. *You're leaving me?* he'd asked.

Shared vulnerability.

Air stuttered into Lori's lungs and she stopped running to stand still, flummoxed by her thoughts. Melissa and Wyatt flashed in her mind. That same anguished expression on Wyatt's face when he was watching over Melissa in the hospital. Lori, just this morning, begging her half sister to let her husband take care of her.

At the same time rejecting the caring that the man she herself loved wanted to give—to share—with her.

A sudden, new certainty burst upon her like another blast of warm, chinook wind. Lori glanced about quickly, trying to get her bearings. Would it be quicker to run back home and get her car or just head to the Anderson, Inc., office from here?

Because she had to go to Josh. She couldn't, shouldn't give him up. Her heart lifting, she assessed that she was just a couple of blocks from the old schoolhouse that housed the office. Picking up her pace once more, she turned the next corner and sped forward.

Josh. She had to ask his forgiveness. She had to make him see that she knew she was wrong. That by choosing to leave him she'd nearly let David win.

"Lori!"

It was as if just thinking his name caused him to materialize. Lori heard her own name called out in a familiar, almost friendly voice. Her feet tripped, and she nearly pitched forward.

"Lori!"

She caught herself and straightened, her body going ice-cold as she saw the slender blond man leaning against the nondescript car across the street. *Oh, God.*

David Post smiled pleasantly. "I got tired of waiting at that high school, so I've been driving around town looking for you," he said.

Lori glanced about. This short block dead-ended into downtown Whitehorn's main street, but the lots on either side of her and David were vacant. From here she could even see cars tooling along the main thoroughfare, people going to the shops and businesses of Whitehorn. And, as the crow flew, even Josh's office was close, but there was no reason for him or anyone to venture into this deserted area.

"What do you want, David?" Lori spoke the words slowly, sizing up the situation. If she ran, he was close enough that he would easily overtake her before she made it to the populated street—she knew how quick he was—but that was also why she'd taken those self-defense classes. There was no reason to panic.

David smiled again. "It's you, Lori. It's always been you." Then he lifted the hand at his side and pointed a gun at her.

Josh hadn't budged from the office's reception area since Lori had left. After pressing some bills on the uniformed kid, he'd gone to stand by the window. He stood there still, his head pounding, his stomach roiling, the kind of sour taste in his mouth that he only associated with a bad hangover. And just as he had the few times he'd felt this lousy, he wanted to go back in time and undo his stupidity.

But you could never reverse a night of overimbibing. You could never take back the words that had let the woman you loved get away.

The front door swung open and Josh jerked his head around, hoping—

But it wasn't Lori walking over the threshold. Instead, it was her half sister Melissa, followed by Wyatt. Their concerned expressions turned alarmed the instant they caught sight of him.

He must look like hell.

Not surprising, because that's exactly where he deserved to go.

Melissa hurried toward him, holding out one hand. Knowing now that she was Lori's half sister, the older woman's beauty only made him miss *his* Southern beauty more.

"What's the matter, Josh?" Melissa asked.

"What's happened?" She touched his forearm, then patted his shoulder, as if convincing herself he was still all there.

Josh rubbed a hand over his face. "Lori's gone."

Wyatt came up behind his wife and laid his palm on her shoulder. "Gone where?"

"Gone, gone." Josh tried swallowing down the taste in his mouth. "I told her I don't love her."

Melissa winced. "You're an idiot," she said, though her kind tone didn't take out the sting.

"You can't call me anything I haven't called myself," he answered. He swiped his face again. "I can't believe I let her get away." Just as he had with Kay, he'd swallowed his misgivings, he'd held back on his need to protect Lori, he'd given her the freedom she wanted.

"She was only trying to protect you, you know." Melissa said.

"What?" Puzzled, Josh looked down at her. "Protect *me?*"

"Remember how she told me to be careful? How she told me to let Wyatt take care of me?"

"Yeah, I remember," Josh answered. "So you'd think she'd take her own advice and let *me* take care of *her.*"

Melissa shook her head. "That's not the way love works, silly. Lori's first instinct was to shield *you.*"

Josh blinked, then lifted his arms from his sides. "Melissa, let's get serious here. I'm six-five, 220 pounds. If we want to determine who makes the better shield, I think we can all agree—"

"You're an idiot, Josh Anderson," Melissa said again, this time not as kindly. She jammed her hands on her hips. "For goodness sake, how many times do we have to tell you male dimwits that size doesn't matter?"

Wyatt looked like he was holding back a grin, but then his face sobered. "Maybe we should argue about that later, my love." He glanced at Josh. "Do you think Lori's in real danger from this ex-husband of hers? Should we call the sheriff's office?"

Lori's ex-husband. The sheriff. The words rubbed like salt against the raw wound that was Josh's soul. "Hell, I don't know what to do," he told Wyatt. "Lori said she was leaving town. That should throw off the bastard."

Melissa's face froze. "She probably went home to pack her things," she said, turning to look at Wyatt.

Her husband's hand squeezed her shoulder, but his gaze went to Josh. "That's why we came. Rick Weber talked to the blond man, too."

Josh frowned. "Wily Rick Weber?"

Wyatt nodded. "He came out earlier today to work up a landscape bid at the Hip Hop. A few minutes ago he stopped by to drop it off and he told us a blond man had asked him about Lori when he was outside the café this morning." Wyatt hesitated. "And Rick had made it his business to find out where Lori lives when she first showed up in town."

Josh's heart stopped. "He told him."

Wyatt nodded. "So—"

But Josh didn't hear any more, because he was sprinting for the door. "I've got to find her."

With one hand he groped for the car keys in his pocket while he pulled open the front door with the other. The springlike air washed over him, its warmth incongruous against his cold determination. He wasn't going to swallow anything anymore, least of all a threat to Lori. He'd start at her apartment. But no matter what it took, he was going to find her.

No matter what it took, he was going to tell her he loved her. That he couldn't stop loving her.

He dashed toward the parking lot, the soles of his boots skidding on the gravel. Even with the skittery noise of the pebbles beneath his feet, though, he heard it.

A gunshot.

His heart jolted. Without a second's hesitation, he switched directions, racing toward the sound. He vaguely heard Wyatt shout from behind him, but Josh didn't slow.

He didn't know how he knew, but he did.

Lori was hurt.

His strides ate up the half block to the nearest intersection. He flew across the road in the direction of Anders Street, dodging a car that protested with a blaring horn.

Josh could only hear his heartbeat in his ears.

He could only see a crumpled figure lying in the street a hundred feet away. Lori, her hair spread out around her. A blond man bending over her.

As Josh pounded toward the two, the man looked

up. It all happened in an instant that seemed to stretch for hours. He started to rise, then Josh was there, grabbing him by the upper arms. Josh lifted the other man off his feet and dragged him away from Lori. His arm slid over the thinner man's chest and Josh gripped the stranger against his body, his gaze on Lori.

"Honey? Lori?" He shouted at her, because her eyes were closed and he needed to wake her up.

The other man was thrashing about and talking, but Josh just hitched him tighter against himself. "Lori!" he yelled again.

Sirens sounded. Wyatt and Melissa rushed up, both bending over Lori's curled, quiescent figure.

Melissa's eyes were wide with alarm when she looked up. "Josh, she's been shot."

Chapter Fourteen

The fluorescent light in the hospital room emitted a steady, high-pitched buzz that sounded like a cricket on helium. It put Josh's teeth on edge, but what the hell, it matched the rest of him.

His butt was on the edge of the chair beside the hospital bed. His nerves were on edge. His life was riding the fine edge between relief and despair.

He leaned toward the still figure covered by a sheet and then a hospital blanket. "Wake up," he whispered. "Please, Lori, I'm just asking for you to open your eyes."

And then, as if she'd heard his request—as if it were the first time he'd asked and not the hundred-and-first—her lashes fluttered. Josh curled his fingers into fists, willing himself to patience.

The most beautiful blue he'd ever seen in his entire life was the blue of Lori's half-open eyes. Though his nerves were still guitar-string tight, he smiled. "Hi," he said softly. "The doctors promised me you'd wake up, but I admit I was getting a little antsy."

They'd also promised to call Security earlier that day, when Josh had insisted on being allowed into Lori's room. Thanks to Dr. Noah Martin's influence, the nurses had finally relented. But they'd threatened Josh with instant eviction if he distressed her in any way.

Lori's gaze darted this way and that, her brow wrinkling in obvious confusion. Josh instantly covered her free hand with his, squeezing lightly. "You're in the Whitehorn Memorial Hospital."

"What?" The word came out a whisper.

Josh squeezed her fingers again, wishing he could shelter her from the truth. "Do you remember what happened this morning, Lori?"

She blinked again, then she froze. "David." She shifted against the sheets, trying to sit up.

"No!" He grasped her right shoulder and pressed it gently back, then forced a calmer note in his voice. "He's in the sheriff's custody. He can't hurt you."

David Post was lucky that the authorities had appeared on the scene so quickly. When Melissa had said Lori'd been shot, Josh had become enraged at the piece of human garbage he'd pulled off her, still struggling in his grip. The timely arrival of the deputies meant that they hadn't had to pull Josh off David. Once the other man was handcuffed, Josh had thought only of Lori.

Now, seeing her awake, he swallowed. "You scared me," he said. "You scared me bad."

Lori's hand turned in his. Her fingers were cold, but her grasp strong. "He had a gun," she said, her voice rough and anxious. "Josh, I remember he had a gun."

There didn't seem to be enough air in the room, just thinking about it. Only the fact that she was here, breathing, awake, kept him sane. "I know, honey. And he...he shot you."

Lori jerked back, then winced. Her head turned and she looked down at her casted left arm. "I remember it burned," she said, "but I didn't realize he'd actually pulled the trigger."

"He did." Josh ran his hand over her hair. "But the gun was found some distance away. We don't know if he tossed it aside, or—"

"I kicked it out of his hand," Lori said.

"You what?"

Lori's brow furrowed. "He was coming closer, holding the gun, talking to me in that cool way he has."

Josh saw her swallow, hard, and he continued stroking her hair to reassure her. "Then what happened?"

She let out a small, mirthless laugh. "I thought how ironic it was. I thought about all those miles I've run, all those self-defense classes I've taken. They weren't any good against a *gun.*"

Josh's gut clenched, the echo of her fear making him sick. "Hell, Lori," he said. He brought her hand to his lips and pressed his mouth against her knuckles. "Hell."

Her gaze focused beyond him, as if she was reliving the moments. "As he came closer, I got really mad about that. That he'd bested me *again*. That no matter what I did, no matter where I went, I couldn't seem to take care of myself."

Her eyes focused on Josh's face. "When he lifted the gun a little higher, I knew what was going to happen next. I heard it go off. This acrid smell filled my nose. I felt that burning. But my anger focused on the gun." She half smiled. "I guess those kick-boxing classes really work."

Josh struggled to breathe. The truth was worse than the picture his imagination had painted. Hellishly worse. "Oh, God, Lori." The words finally pushed past his tight throat. "Oh, God."

Her brows came together. "Josh? What's wrong? You told me that the sheriff has David. You told me I'm going to be okay." She stilled. "You're all right, aren't you? And Melissa? He didn't hurt—"

"No, no," Josh quickly reassured her. "Everyone is fine." He closed his eyes. "That's a lie. I'm not fine. Physically, yes. But I have to be honest. Now. For the first time. Lori, I don't think I'll ever be the same again."

She was shifting against the sheets again, grimacing.

"No," he said. "Don't move." Taking a deep

breath, he fumbled for the bed's controls and pushed the button to lift her head. "Lori, I—"

"Is he bothering you?" A nurse bustled into the room, her gaze for Lori, her disapproval for Josh. "And when, pray tell, did you wake up?"

"Just a few minutes ago," Lori answered, then darted a glance at him. "And Josh isn't bothering me."

The nurse matter-of-factly disengaged their hands to check Lori's pulse. "He's been bothering me," she grumbled. "From the moment you arrived at the hospital."

In a few efficient moments she'd checked Lori's vital signs, settled her more comfortably, lifted a bent straw stuck in a glass of water to her lips. Then, with one last sniff in Josh's direction and vague threats of calling the doctor, she left the room.

The activity appeared to have worn Lori out. Josh swallowed, the sight of her pale, beautiful features clawing at his heart. He straightened in his chair. "Maybe you should get some rest."

"Don't leave me." Lori blinked, as if her own words surprised her.

Josh wondered how many ups and downs a man could survive in one day. He leaned toward her, needing to be close. "I wasn't going anywhere, honey. I'm...not sure I can."

At the small, puzzled shake of her head, Josh made himself continue. "Not, not until you hear me out anyway." He found her free hand again, slipping his fingers between hers. "I'm so sorry for what I said to you this morning at the office. For lying to you as I did. I was operating strictly out of the fear of losing you, but instead of what I really wanted to say, I let you get away. I pushed you away."

Lori, no surprise, latched onto the most important point first. "Expand on this lying part."

Leaning forward and resting his elbows on the mattress, he lifted her hand and cupped it between both of his. He'd prayed like this while she was sleeping, and his heart was not much less anxious now. "I'll go slow, Lori. I'll wait. I'll give you whatever space, whatever room you need. But I need you to know that I love you. And I think…I want…I know we could have something together. Someday. When you're ready."

Pink tinged the paleness of Lori's cheeks. "Josh, I—"

Before she could say any more, the surgeon pushed through the door, the nurse a step behind him. It was the nurse who gave Josh his walking papers, of course, and he reluctantly left Lori, only to hover outside the closed door to her room.

Though she felt as if every bone and muscle in her body was throbbing, after Lori spoke with the doctor she asked the nurse to see if Josh was anywhere nearby. In a moment the other woman stuck her head back in. "Is six inches away 'nearby' enough for you?" she asked, rolling her eyes. "Any closer and I would have beaned him with the door."

Josh pushed past the white-smocked woman, his gaze on Lori. "Did you need me?"

Oh, she did. He strode into the room, and it was as if she hadn't seen him in months instead of minutes. But everything about Josh was so dear—and wouldn't he hate that word, too? The thought would have made her laugh, if it didn't make her heart ache so.

Did she deserve such dearness? Such niceness? He said he loved her—and that wonder was still sinking in—but could she bring her troubled past into his life again? Because she knew, better than anyone, that David Post wasn't going to melt away. At best, there would be interviews with the sheriff and court dates and parole hearings. Months of them. Years.

"Josh, I—"

The door to her room swung open again, and half grateful for the interruption, Lori looked toward it. Melissa peeked in, her face worried.

Her gaze found Lori's, and the expression eased. "You're awake!"

"And alive," Lori added. It was a truth that made it necessary to tell all the other truths, she thought with sudden clarity. As weary as she was, as unsure about the future, she still beckoned Melissa in. "I need to talk to you, too."

When Josh made to give Melissa his chair, she waved him back and perched on the edge of Lori's bed. "First," the older woman said. "Tell me you're going to be all right. Then—"

Lori held up her hand. "I'm going to be fine. But

first, first I need to tell *you* something." Inhaling a long breath didn't help ease her nervousness. "I've never told you the entire reason I came to White-horn," she said, her gaze on Melissa's face. "Yes, it was where my mother was born and raised, and yes, I was interested in seeing the town. But I was…more interested in seeing my half sister."

Melissa's eyes widened. "You mean…?"

Lori swallowed. "I'm sorry. I don't know how this will make you feel about your father, but even though I never knew him, he was my father too. I have some proof. Letters—"

"That won't be necessary," Melissa said slowly. Her gaze ran over Lori's features. "All the proof I need is right in front of me. I'm just surprised I didn't figure it out before. My father wasn't known for his faithfulness, Lori, I've known that for years. And since you first came to town, people have commented over and over on how much we look alike."

"Maybe I should have been honest from the be-ginning," Lori admitted. "But I didn't want you to feel obligated in any way toward me. I didn't want you to feel that we *had* to have a relationship."

Melissa smiled. "But we both felt something right away, yes?"

The tightness in Lori's chest halfway eased. "Yes. But I also have to confess that I…that I wanted badly to establish a relationship with you. With my mother gone and David—well, you know about David now—I needed all the strength I could muster. And I thought rebuilding my life with the foundation of a family might make me stronger.''

Melissa's smile was tender. Her hand found Lori's and she grasped it firmly. ''We will make you strong. I promise you that.''

Hot tears stung the corners of Lori's eyes as she looked at their joined hands. She remembered the first time Melissa had covered her hand, when they'd first met at the Five & Dime weeks ago. ''I promise to be a good friend to you, too,'' she whispered.

Tears glistened in Melissa's eyes as well. ''Sisters,'' she corrected. ''We're sisters, and we'll give and take.''

Give and take. The three words sank into Lori's consciousness, then into her heart, then deeper, into her soul. Without letting go of Melissa, she turned her head toward Josh. ''I have things to tell you, too.''

The legs of his chair squeaked against the linoleum floor as he slid closer to her. His dark-brown eyes were as serious as she'd ever seen them. ''Go ahead.''

But she was too cowardly to start with the most important thing first. ''The last time that David hurt me, I ended up in a hospital room just like this one. As the nurses bustled in and out, I made a vow. I promised myself that I wasn't going to be weak again.''

Josh nodded. ''The running, the kickboxing, those self-defense moves you know.''

''Yes. I worked so hard to be strong.'' She sucked in a breath. ''And then…and then David had that gun.

I'd never prepared for that. Never expected I'd have to be…''

"Superwoman?" Melissa supplied.

Lori sighed. "Exactly. So all my preparation, all my desire to stand on my own two feet couldn't make me…"

"Bulletproof," Melissa offered again.

With a little laugh, Lori looked over at the other woman. "This sister stuff is working out really well."

Melissa smiled back. "Told you."

Lori returned her gaze to Josh. "So when I was standing there, facing David all alone, I told you I was mad. But I also wanted to scream with frustration because I thought I'd never get a chance to tell you…" She hesitated.

"That—" Melissa started.

"I love you, Josh." She threw her sister an amused glance. "See, I was going to get it out."

"Just making sure," Melissa answered mildly. "Anything else you have to tell him?"

"Yes." Lori risked a peek at Josh, who was sitting frozen, as if her words had stunned him. "I want to spend the rest of my life with you."

That's when her big, brawny Josh appeared ready to crumble. His shoulders slumped, his face paled, his eyes turned even darker. "Say that again?" he said hoarsely.

"I love you, Josh. I want to marry you."

His big body lurched toward her. Lori slipped her hand from Melissa's and held Josh off. "Wait. There's something else."

He settled back in his chair, his body radiating leashed energy, though his face was wary. "Nothing else matters," he said.

Lori licked her lips. "The truth matters. The whole truth." She hesitated. "Josh, I also have to say that I'm not sure whether if I went back to live this morning over that I'd do anything different."

He opened his mouth to protest, but she held out her hand again. "Let me finish. You need to know that I still will find it hard to put you at risk for my sake. That might make me foolhardy in your eyes, but that's the truth."

Josh found her hand and lifted it, holding it against his face. "You were trying to protect me."

Lori relaxed a little, cheered by his understanding.

"Just like I wanted to protect you." He smiled at her. "Don't you see? I can understand that. Just as I expect that you can understand I wanted to take care of you, too."

Give and take. Lori looked at the man she loved, feeling his warmth, his goodness, flowing down her arm and toward her heart. Still, there was her past, and David, and... She bit her lip. "What if..."

"You just shut up and grab for happiness?" Melissa said. She crossed her arms over her chest and gave Lori a stern look. "I'm the big sister, right?"

At Lori's nod, she continued. "Well that means you have to listen to me. And I tell you, from experience, mind you, that what-ifs are a waste of time."

Lori remembered Melissa telling her about her marriage to Wyatt and how they'd been separated by circumstances for a number of years. "But—"

"But nothing." It was Josh who finished for Lori this time. "What-ifs *are* a waste of time. It's what will be that we should be talking about. Looking forward to."

Tears were gathering in Lori's eyes again. "A partnership," she said, as one spilled over to run hotly down her cheek.

Josh smiled, then closed his eyes, as if savoring the moment. "A marriage."

A week later, when her arm was on the mend but still in a sling, Josh convinced Lori to go for a drive with him on Sunday afternoon. The chinook winds had left as quickly as they had come, and the Montana winter cold was back, though the streets were still without snow.

Lori snuggled back in her seat, wrapped in an old coat of Josh's. She'd moved in with him until their wedding in March. Neither one of them wanted to waste a moment apart.

"Close your eyes," he suddenly commanded.

Surprised, Lori looked over at him. "What?"

"I want you to close your eyes."

"Why?"

"Humor me," Josh answered, with a grin. "Close your eyes until I tell you to open them."

With a shrug, Lori obediently shut her eyes. Humoring Josh was turning out to be one of the most pleasant ways to spend her time. As a matter of fact, she'd just humored him that morning, lying back on their bed—he was still so worried about her arm—while he made delirious love to her.

The car braked to a stop. "Can I open my eyes now?" she asked.

"Nope. Keep them closed. I'll help you out."

And he did just that. Careful not to jar her injury, he moved her from the car and then urged her to walk forward. "What's this all about?" she asked, but he refused to answer.

The snick of a latch and the sudden rush of warm air told her a door had opened in front of them. Lori thought she could feel the presence of other people, and she sniffed, smelling the delicious scent of warm food and something else familiar.

"Melissa?" she called out. "I smell your perfume."

Josh bent to her ear. "You can look now," he said.

Lori's eyes popped open. Then her mouth dropped.

They were standing in the half-finished Hip Hop. The drywall was up, but her feet were still on the subfloor. In the place where the café's tables and booths would one day be, there were several long portable tables filled with food. Portable heaters were placed strategically, too. And the restaurant was full of people.

A banner reading Welcome to the Family, Lori! was stretched across one blank wall.

Her throat tightened, and she reached out to clutch Josh's hand. "What's going on?"

He pulled her close. "A party, honey. A party for you."

Hand-in-hand with Wyatt, Melissa approached, her smile so dazzling that Lori thought it might blind her. "I wanted everyone to meet you."

Lori's gaze roamed around the room, noting mostly familiar faces. "I know these people," she said, puzzled.

"Not in this way." Melissa reached out to tuck a strand of hair behind Lori's ear. "Come meet my friends, little sister."

Lori's heart tripled in size. She looked up at Josh, and he grinned. She saw a matching one stretch across Wyatt's face.

All over the room, people were smiling. Smiling at her. Welcoming her to Whitehorn and into their lives.

A shiver of pure happiness, pure as Montana air, rushed over her skin. She was part of a family. Part of this town.

"Thank you," she said to Melissa. "Thank you," Lori called out to all the happy faces around her.

Then she turned to Josh, her passionate, patient partner. "Thank you." The sound of a champagne cork popping made her laugh out loud.

The sound signified her future. And, as for her past…it wasn't her weakness any longer. She knew that. It was what made her exalt in this moment. It was what made her cherish Josh. It was what made her better able to appreciate her love for him and their great good luck that they'd found each other.

*   *   *   *   *

The next MONTANA *story is out in February 2003.*